T574g

....The Great Skinner Homestead....

Also by Stephanie S. Tolan

........The Great........ Skinner ....Homestead........

Stephanie S. Tolan

FOUR WINDS PRESS
New York

Four Winds Press
Macmillan Publishing Company
866 Third Avenue, New York, NY 10022
Collier Macmillan Canada, Inc.
First Edition
Printed in the United States of America

10 9 8 7 6 5 4 3 2 1

The text of this book is set in 11 point Primer.

Library of Congress Cataloging-in-Publication Data
Tolan, Stephanie S.
The great Skinner homestead / Stephanie S. Tolan.
—1st ed.   p.   cm.
Summary: Fifteen-year-old Jenny relates her
family's misadventures homesteading in the
Adirondack Mountains during the summer.
ISBN 0-02-789362-6
[1. Family life—Fiction. 2. Mountain life—Fiction.
3. Adirondack Mountains (N.Y.)—Fiction.]   I. Title.
PZ7.T5735Grdg 1988   [Fic]—dc19
88-3970   CIP   AC

To O. Franklin Kenworthy,
Friend and Good Person—
Memories will never be enough.

.... Contents ....

....The Great Skinner Homestead....

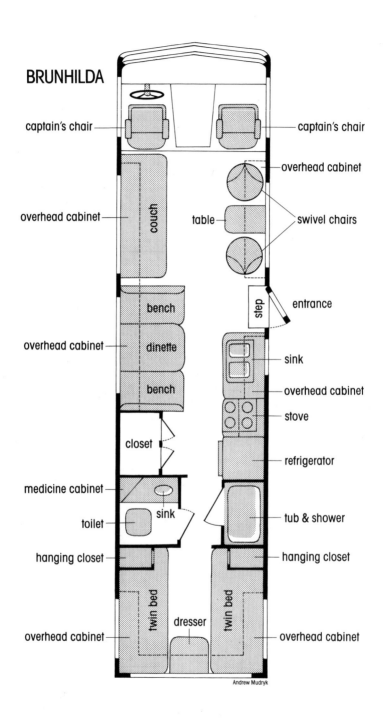

BRUNHILDA

captain's chair

captain's chair

overhead cabinet

couch

table

swivel chairs

overhead cabinet

bench

dinette

overhead cabinet

bench

step

entrance

sink

overhead cabinet

stove

closet

refrigerator

medicine cabinet

sink

toilet

tub & shower

hanging closet

hanging closet

twin bed

twin bed

dresser

overhead cabinet

overhead cabinet

Andrew Mudryk

.... Prologue ....

(Yes, This Is Important!)

It's me again, Jenny Skinner. Writing books about my family is getting to be a habit with me. It's the way I cope with being a Skinner. Even on the worst days, I can always think that someday a reader—like you—will know about what I've gone through and sympathize, and it helps.

This book should be done right, because my friend Sarah gave me *How to Write a Marketable Book* for my sixteenth birthday (which you'll read about later on), and I've tried to do what the author says. Except when I disagree with him.

If you haven't read any of my other books, you don't need to read them now. All you need for background information is this prologue. But if you've already read *The Great Skinner Getaway*, you're allowed to skip ahead to the first chapter.

There are six human members of the Skinner family. Our mother, Eleanor Jean Woodford Skinner, once went on strike against the rest of us, totally disrupting our normal, middle-class existence, and causing me to write my first book. Mom is fairly small, sort of "cute," quite tough and—once her strike was over—relatively sane and reliable.

Our father, Michael Richard Skinner, went from almost stodgily sane to almost completely nuts when he lost his job and started his own business, At Your Service, which was so successful that it nearly destroyed us all. Luckily, he had the good sense to sell the business. But then he used the proceeds from the sale to buy a used thirty-five-foot-long motor home, which we named *Brunhilda*. It was his idea to take off in *Brunhilda* for a "getaway" this summer. Like the business, our getaway didn't turn out exactly as he'd expected.

There are four Skinner offspring. I'm the oldest and am utterly normal (except that this is the fourth book I've written since I was fourteen). I have a boyfriend (Jason) and a best friend I've already mentioned (Sarah).

Next comes Ben. He's an athletic, mechanically gifted, fourteen-year-old loner with a passion for computers. Then there's Marcia. She's a neat, well-organized, violin-playing person whose body is almost twelve, but whose mind is closing in on thirty. The youngest Skinner is Rick, who's nearly ten and won't let us refer to him anymore as the baby. He's nice, a little flaky, and an animal lover.

We brought our part golden retriever (Buffy), Rick's Siamese cat (Chatter), and our old gray Persian cat (Czar Nicholas) along with us on our getaway. Rick also has two rats, but we left them at home with a rat-sitter, so they don't come into this story.

As we begin, the time is mid-July. The setting is the wilds of the Adirondack Mountains in the state of New York, where *Brunhilda* has broken an axle in a deep trench that stretches all the way across a narrow dirt road, where a large motor home should never have been in the first place. (Don't ask.) This accident has stranded the Skinner family far from the nearest civilization, but quite close to the ancient log cabin and extremely primitive homestead of one Minnie Berry, an eighty-five-year-old retired schoolteacher with a touch of arthritis and a wicked tongue.

Going home is impossible, because a family from Ohio is renting our house till the first of September. So Mom and Dad, in one of their moments of madness, have just decided that we should spend the rest of the summer helping Miss Berry tend her "place," as she calls it. We assume this will mean a nice, quiet mountain vacation with an occasional brief stint of gardening. We are about to learn otherwise.

.... On the Level ....

"Up, up, up!"

Sound filtered into my dream. Groggily, I opened my eyes. I didn't want to be awake. There had been a red BMW in that dream.

I closed my eyes again. The car had been a present for my sixteenth birthday, and I wanted it back! I reached for my pillow, wanting to snuggle back to sleep before the BMW vanished forever. No pillow. I started to stretch my legs but couldn't. My feet were jammed against something.

I opened my eyes again. During the night *Brunhilda* must have tilted even farther into the trench in which she'd broken her front axle. I'd slipped so far down in bed that if my sheet hadn't been firmly tucked in at the bottom, I'd have been on the floor by now. Czar Nicholas, a fat, furry sleeping presence, was hot against the small of my back. Heavy as he was, he seemed to be trying to push me even farther.

Brunhilda shuddered, Buffy yelped, and I remembered what had awakened me. Dad, yelling. Now he was making his way uphill toward the bathroom from the fold-out sofa bed in the living room where he and Mom sleep. *Brunhilda* vibrated with his every step. "Up, up, up!" he yelled again, as the door to the bathroom slammed shut. "Rise and shine!"

4

Marcia, jammed by gravity against the wall, and as far down the slope of her bed as I was down mine, groaned. Then she clawed her way up to her pillow and buried her face in it, holding on to the edge of the mattress to keep herself from sliding. "If id moh deen eb?" was what I heard.

"What?"

She lifted her head. "Is it morning yet?"

I waved in the direction of the windows. Pale light was coming in, between the slats in the blinds. "Technically."

"I thought this was supposed to be vacation," she grumbled.

By the time I'd untangled myself from my sheets and sat up, Dad was out of the bathroom and beginning one of his early-morning pep talks. There is nothing—*nothing*—more annoying than to begin a day being told how much work has to be done. Though we have told him and told him this, Dad pays no attention.

"On your feet, you slugabeds!" he yelled. "There's lots to do today. Time is flying. Rise and shine. Up and at 'em!"

Ben groaned. Marcia groaned. I groaned. Rick, who likes mornings, jumped down from the ceiling bunk in the living room. The *thump* rocked *Brunhilda* and jarred my back teeth. I sat still. There are two good bathroom choices in *Brunhilda*. Get in first, which means having to get up before everybody else but lets you have a few ounces of hot water, or wait till everybody else is done, which leaves you only cold water but lets you stay in bed longer. I'd already missed first place, so I decided to hold out for last.

"What do you suppose he means by lots to do?" I asked. Marcia only groaned again.

Now that I was sitting up, I was no longer acting as a backstop for Czar Nicholas. Still sleeping, he began to slip gently down the bed. As he moved, he picked up momentum, slipping faster and faster. Just as he was going over the edge, he opened one green eye. A tangle of cat and sheet thudded onto the floor. There was a slight pause, then a brief struggle. The bundle slid along the floor until it bumped into the wall. Another brief struggle. Then silence. The deep rumble of his purr filled our tiny bedroom. The end of his fluffy gray tail and one ear could be seen poking up from the sheet. He had gone back to sleep. What I wouldn't give to have that cat's approach to life.

There was a blue gray mist between the ground and the lowest branches of the pine trees when Dad gathered us outside a short time later. The mist was clammy, but the air was reasonably comfortable. We didn't question this or even think about it. We did not know that high in the Adirondacks in upstate New York on a mid-July morning before seven it should have been at least chilly, maybe even cold. Not being in touch with the outside world, we had not yet heard the words "record-breaking heat wave."

Considering that Dad hadn't had any coffee yet (the coffee pot had slid off the stove), he was pretty cheerful. "Obviously, we cannot go so much as another day—or night—living on the tilt. The first thing we're going to do is get *Brunhilda* level."

"Before breakfast?" Rick asked.

"Before breakfast," Dad said.

"But I'm starving!" Rick doesn't eat a large *variety* of foods, but he does eat large amounts.

Dad smiled, but the edges of his mouth were very tight. "And I have not had my coffee. But it's good to do a little physical work before breakfast. Farm kids always do their chores first thing."

"But we aren't farm—" Rick started.

"As soon as we're finished, I'll fix pancakes," Mom put in quickly. "And bacon." Rick was satisfied with this.

"*Brunhilda* is our home," Dad went on. "And since she is at this moment all but uninhabitable, she comes first. We will fix her up—quickly—eat breakfast and then have a family meeting. I have a surprise for all of you."

This announcement was greeted with a pained silence. Dad's family meetings are bad enough. His surprises tend to be catastrophic.

Dad frowned. "Don't look at me that way. You'll like this. You really will!"

Mom smiled warily. I suspected that even she wasn't in on this one. Marcia rolled her eyes and shrugged.

"Okay now, first things first," Dad said, his voice charged with enthusiasm. "Your mother will help me jack *Brunhilda* up, while you kids gather flat rocks. Lots of them. We're going to build up a sort of wall—a platform for *Brunhilda* to rest on."

"Why can't we just jack her up till she's level?" I asked.

Dad shook his head. "Because we only have one jack. She needs support under both front wheels—requiring two jacks—or else all the way across—requiring this platform."

"But—"

"I know what I'm doing, Jenny. Now, everybody, go find rocks. And be sure they're *flat!*"

So, while Mom and Dad wrestled with the huge jack that had come with *Brunhilda*, we kids, uncheerfully, set to work.

Rick, spurred by hunger, got his backpack so he could carry all the rocks he was sure he'd find, and set off into the woods with Buffy bounding eagerly at his side. Marcia, ever methodical, got out her rock and mineral field book to see what kind of rock would be best. "So much for fishing," Ben muttered, and stomped off in the general direction of the trout stream.

I started looking right there, in the woods next to *Brunhilda*. Finding flat rocks, I was sure, would be easy. After all, mountains are made of rock.

It wasn't long before I discovered that the rock mountains are made of is not the kind of rock you can just pick up and carry around. It tends to come in Brontosaurus-size chunks. Whole trees grow in its cracks.

Where there are smaller rocks, they tend to be hidden under dead leaves and moss and old branches. You find these by tripping over them. Then, if you try to pick them up, you discover they are much bigger than they looked, and set in cement. Occasionally, if you're lucky, you can dig around one with a stick (or your fingernails, until they're all broken off) and actually pry it up. However, no rock you get this way is flat. Ever.

After a very long and nearly fruitless search, when I was so far into the woods I could barely hear Mom and Dad cursing *Brunhilda* and the jack, Ben hollered from the stream. He'd found tons of flat rocks along the banks. Marcia took her book with her, to make sure they were the right kind of rocks, and she and Ben and I started hauling them back.

Soon the temperature that had been comfortable while we were just standing around, got warmer. A little while after I noticed it was getting warm, I noticed it was more like hot. Very hot. The rocks were heavy. And the distance between *Brunhilda* and the trout stream kept getting longer and longer. "Vacation," I heard Marcia say as she staggered past with another load.

When Rick finally appeared, he was dragging his backpack behind him, a triumphant grin on his pink and sweaty face. "I found a whole bunch. I bet I have more than anybody—seventy-eight!" he announced.

I looked at his pack. It was full all right, but seventyeight? I was barely able to carry four at a time.

Rick unzipped his pack and dumped it proudly at Dad's feet. There *were* seventy-eight. And they were flat. But you wouldn't call them rocks. They were stones—skipping stones—about two inches across. Pretty. Smooth. And useless. Dad yelled. Rick, who is very sensitive, cried. Not long afterward he and Buffy disappeared into the woods again.

The rest of us—including Mom and Dad, who had finally gotten *Brunhilda* jacked up—went on hauling. When we finally had what Dad thought was a big enough pile of rocks, Dad and Ben climbed down into the trench to start stacking them.

This was not as easy as Dad had expected. Rocks are not like bricks, all square and even. Some are thick on one end and thin on the other. Some are flat on one side and bumpy on the other. There are narrow ones and wide ones, skinny ones and fat ones. Furthermore, the bottom of the trench was uneven. And muddy. Dad and Ben would put some rocks down, put a couple more on top, and while they were reaching for more, the ones on top would slide off. Dad blamed Ben for doing it wrong; Ben blamed me or Marcia for handing him the wrong rocks.

Twice, after he and Ben had actually gotten a good start, Dad stood back with his hands on his hips to survey the work, shook his head, and tore it down again, heaving the rocks back where they'd been before we'd lifted them down to him. We did not care for this. Mom had a quiet little talk with him the second time he did it, and though we couldn't hear what she said, his answer was loud and clear. "Eleanor, a job worth doing is worth doing well." Then he added that if she thought she could do better, she was welcome to come stand in the trench and darned well do it. Mom and Dad didn't talk a whole lot after that.

We had to go back to the creek for more rocks several times, but finally the job was done. A fairly straight, fairly even wall of rock filled the center of the trench, just under *Brunhilda's* wounded front. With careful stacking and wedging, and some sticks to serve as braces, the boulder in the middle—the one that had broken the axle in the first place—had been made a part of the wall.

Dad wiped the sweat from his face, leaving dirt streaks. Ben did the same. They both smiled. They climbed out of the trench to assess their work and patted each other on the back. All arguments were forgotten.

"That's done it!"

"I'm starving!" Rick wailed from the woods.

Dad went over to the jack. "Now, all we do is lower her onto her platform and—voilà!—she will be level."

Marcia crouched down and surveyed the top of the wall. "Doesn't look too sturdy to me," she whispered. I shushed her.

Dad began cranking *Brunhilda* down. As she got closer and closer to the wall, I held my breath. I was hot, I was tired, and I was hungry. There was a *clunk*, and Dad lowered the jack the rest of the way and pulled it out. *Brunhilda* was actually resting on the wall. I started breathing again.

We were done. Rick came out of the woods. "Hurray!" he said. And then there was a low sound—a heavy, grating sort of groan. Instinctively, we all stepped back. *Brunhilda* lurched slightly and, like a giant spitting watermelon seeds, popped one rock after another across the trench. In a matter of moments, she was right back where she started from. "Does this mean I don't get my pancakes?" Rick asked.

.... The Surprise ....

What we had for breakfast was cereal, in those little boxes that you can just cut open and pour milk into. We ate these outside, next to the trench full of flat rocks that weren't a wall anymore. We sat there on the ground, hot, sweaty, and quiet, shoveling soggy flakes into our mouths as fast as we could, while milk dripped steadily onto our laps. Rick and Ben each ate three boxes, in spite of the fact that after their first ones, only the nutritional kind were left.

Afterward, Dad and Ben decided that the way to solve the problem was not to build a wall for *Brunhilda* to rest on, but to completely fill in the trench. That way, there would be no place for the rocks to move, so they wouldn't. Unfortunately, that way we ran out of rocks very fast. We had to get about a million more.

On the other hand, it wasn't necessary to place each rock as carefully, so filling the trench didn't take very long. Then Ben thought up an intricate arrangement of logs and rocks to put between *Brunhilda*'s front wheels to keep her weight off them. This time, when Dad removed the jack, after a little grating and grumbling, a little settling, *Brunhilda* rested firmly. We waited a few minutes just in case, and then—gently—we cheered.

Brunhilda was level. Czar Nicholas settled himself on the dashboard and peered out at us through the windshield, looking as smug as if he'd done the job himself.

"He seems satisfied," Mom said.

"He's always satisfied," Rick pointed out. Then he looked around. "Where's Chatter? Did somebody let her out?"

None of us had seen Rick's Siamese cat all morning. "Nobody needs to *let* her out," Dad said. "That cat could escape from Alcatraz with three paws tied behind her back."

"Especially if she knew there were small animals out there waiting to be murdered," Ben said.

Rick punched Ben in the shoulder. "Don't say that!"

"It's true," Ben said, punching him back. "And I don't know why you get so upset. It's only nature."

"You don't care," Rick grumped. "Because you kill things, too."

"What things?"

"Fish."

"Oh, right." Ben turned to Mom and Dad. "Can I go fishing now? We could have trout for dinner."

"Family meeting," Dad said.

Everybody groaned. Even Mom. The mist had long ago burned away, and there was no doubt about the temperature. It was hot. Not hot for upstate New York. Not hot for the mountains. Just plain hot! And we'd been slaving away since dawn. We were sweaty. We were dirty. I, for one, was thinking about finding a nice cold lake and spending the rest of the day up to my neck in it.

"Family meeting," Dad repeated more firmly. "I told you, I have a surprise! You'll love it!"

We were, to put it mildly, doubtful. Let me explain that if our parents spent any time reading about how to raise children, they would know how hard and how dangerous it is. They would know that the world is full of children who turn to drugs and alcohol and violence because of what their parents do to them. Like making them attend theoretically democratic family meetings where surprises are announced and kids can't vote.

Mom, detecting signs of impending rebellion, suggested that the meeting should be held by the stream. "That way, we can dangle our feet while you tell us your surprise."

"Can I fish instead of dangling?" Ben asked.

"I don't see why not," Mom answered before Dad could.

Oddly enough, it didn't seem nearly as far from *Brunhilda* to the stream this time. And I hadn't noticed, while we were getting rocks, what a beautiful stream it was. The water was shallow, very clear, and very cold. It was moving pretty fast, over and around the larger rocks and boulders in its path, but not fast enough to make a lot of white water and noise. It just sort of burbled pleasantly. As soon as we got there, Buffy plunged in, rushing first upstream, then down, occasionally shoving her nose into the water, as if to sniff under the edges of the rocks.

Rick immediately kicked off his shoes, stuffed his socks into them, and followed her in. Obviously a great idea. In moments the rest of us were wading. The cold water rushing around my ankles felt wonderful. But the rocks were slippery. Rick took three steps and fell in. He scrambled up, took another couple of steps, and fell again. Finally, he just sat down in the water and let it rush around him.

That looked good to me, so I sat down, too. Fantastic! Marcia was next, then Mom and finally Dad. All of us (except Ben, who was busy scouting up and down the banks, looking for fish) were sitting in the water, clothes and all. This was what a vacation should be! The smell of pine and balsam in the air, brilliant blue sky above, water rushing around and over us, and sunlight glinting on the ripples. Then Dad started talking. You can't have everything. "I've been thinking," he began. This was ominous. "This morning, as I lay on that slanted sofa bed with the blood rushing to my head, I realized something very important. Think about *Brunhilda*. There she is, a class A thirty-five-foot motor home, technologically complex, with a propane refrigerator, a propane stove, a microwave oven, her own plumbing system and electrical generator."

Mom scooped up a handful of water and let it run out between her fingers, sparkling in the sunlight. "Yes, Michael. We all agree that *Brunhilda* is a marvel of modern technology."

"Right. A marvel of modern technology. But she was brought down by a rock. A mere piece of limestone—"

"Granite," Marcia corrected him.

"Whatever. The point is, she's crippled. Practically destroyed."

"Everything still works," Mom protested. "Except, of course, that we can't go anywhere."

"But everything won't work indefinitely. The generator runs on gas. Eventually, we'll be out. Then no more electricity."

"We can always get more gas," Ben pointed out. "There's a station in that town, isn't there? Somebody could hike down."

"Or ride Minnie Berry's mule," Rick said. Dad had done this after *Brunhilda*'s axle broke, looking for a garage.

"Will you let me finish? It isn't just gas. When *Brunhilda*'s waste tank gets full, we won't be able to use the toilet anymore. And when her water tank is empty, the sinks and shower won't work. She may be modern and convenient, but she's terribly vulnerable. And so are we. So is our whole civilization. *Brunhilda* is a symbol."

"Of our whole civilization?" I asked.

"Exactly. Our civilization hangs by a thread." Buffy came bounding toward us, splashing wildly. Dad ignored her. "Do you know what would happen if the electricity suddenly went out—everywhere?"

"Why would it do that?" Rick asked.

"A bomb. Terrorists. It doesn't matter. The point is that without electricity, we'd be lost. No radio or television, no lights, no heat, no traffic signals, no radar for air travel, no computers . . ."

Ben, who was upstream, peering under the edges of the bank for likely fish hideouts, yelped. "No computers?"

"No computers," Dad repeated.

"But our whole world, practically, is based on computers."

"Exactly! That's what I'm saying—"

"Where is this leading, Michael?" Mom, like me, was interested in getting to the surprise part.

"We're spoiled," Dad said. "Not just the Skinner family. Twentieth-century Americans. All spoiled. We couldn't get along without the comforts of technology. We don't know how. We take everything for granted. You want to reach someone, pick up the phone. Stick a plug in the wall and the hair dryer works. Turn on the faucet and water comes out. Flush the toilet—"

"Yes, dear, we get the picture."

"But we have no control over any of it. The city pipes our water to us, treats our sewage. Utility companies make our electricity, phone companies control our access to each other. We're at the mercy of faceless bureaucracies. We buy our food in plastic containers. Our clothes off store racks. We don't have a clue about how to live any other way."

Buffy, apparently tired of wandering up and down the stream, threw herself down and rolled in the water, splashing, so that rainbows danced above her.

Dad shook his fist in the air. "We're ignorant. Dependent." Buffy stood up and bounced over to Dad, wagging her tail. Intent on his speech, he ignored her. "City dwellers in the twentieth century are only seconds away from catastrophe!"

Buffy spread her front feet, planted them solidly, and shook herself from nose to tail.

Dad's shout was probably heard three mountains away, like Swiss yodeling. He jumped to his feet, dripping and sputtering, and we burst out laughing. He'd looked so surprised.

"Maybe she thought you were getting a little hot," Mom said when she caught her breath.

Dad dried his mustache with the collar of his shirt. Buffy had prudently vanished into the shade beneath the trees. He looked at us, we looked back at him. "Maybe I did get a little carried away."

We all nodded solemnly and then cracked up all over again. When everybody was finally quiet, Dad sat back down in the water.

"All right, Michael," Mom said. "Go on. We're listening."

"I am serious, you know. If we had to get along without all that technology—even without electricity—we wouldn't have any idea how to cope. And here's Minnie Berry living up here with her wood stove and her mule and her kerosene lamps, just the way the pioneers did two, three hundred years ago. Independent. In control. Raising her own food. Meeting all her own needs."

"Using an outhouse," I said, and shuddered.

"She's a pioneer. And the world she lives in is simple and clean." Dad waved his arm at the woods around us, at the stream, gurgling in the sunshine. "Look at all this. Isn't this more beautiful than the city? Clean air. Fresh smells. The world the way it's supposed to be."

"Your surprise, Michael," Mom reminded him.

"Okay. Here it is. I've decided that we're going to get away from the trap of civilization. We're going to take control of our lives, learn to survive. Like the pioneers. We're going to move up here, to the last wilderness left in the northeastern United States."

I shook my head, trying to clear whatever it was that was interfering with my hearing. For a moment, I thought he'd said "move up here." I looked at Mom. Her mouth was open. She must have heard it, too.

"Move up here? Permanently?" she asked.

"Of course, permanently. We'll have a little homestead. We'll buy a place—not too big, a few acres. Maybe a stream. We'll fell a few trees, build ourselves a log cabin. It isn't impossible, you know, to be independent. Minnie Berry does it. If she can, we can. We'll be twentieth-century pioneers. We'll manage everything ourselves. Build our own shelter. Raise our own food—hunt, fish. Clean and simple."

"Can we have a mule?" Rick did not seem to grasp the full impact of Dad's idea.

"What about school?" Marcia said. "Where would we go to school?"

"This is the state of New York, Marcia, there is certainly a school. The kids who live up here get bused someplace."

"Someplace," Marcia repeated, horror in her voice.

"Someplace! And what about my violin lessons? What about Madame Ardelle?"

"Madame Ardelle is not the only violin teacher in America," Dad said. Marcia set her jaw and didn't reply.

"Would we have electricity?" Ben asked.

"I suppose we could use a generator. But we'd be ready to do without it, too. We'd heat with a wood stove. We'd have kerosene lamps."

Maybe I was dreaming. I had to be dreaming. One did not abandon a perfectly good two-story frame house in the suburbs of Philadelphia and take up residence in a log cabin! I looked at Mom. She would put a stop to this craziness. She was staring off toward the tops of the trees.

"Slow down a moment," Mom said.

Slow down? What did she mean, slow down? What was wrong with "Michael, you are stark, staring crazy"?

"Do you have a particular place in mind?" she asked.

"No, but I'm sure there's land for sale up here. Adirondack Park has six million acres. It doesn't all belong to the state. People sell land."

"How would we pay for it?"

"We can sell the house. Real estate's gone through the roof back home. What we'd make on the deal would more than cover everything we'd need. With a nice nest egg to boot."

Back home, he'd said. That was the point. Back there was home. This—I looked around. Pretty, yes. Natural, yes. But this was vacation. Only vacation!

"And *you'd* build a log cabin?" Mom asked.

"Simplest kind of construction there is," Dad said, his voice radiating confidence. Or madness. I began to wonder if altitude can affect the brain.

Mom, smiling vaguely, splashed some water toward Dad. "I have a job back home, remember?" Since her strike, Mom has been working as a research assistant for a famous writer.

Dad splashed back at her. "You've been writing that newspaper column since we left. You know how much you've liked it. Why not keep doing it? Maybe syndicate. Think how much more satisfying it would be than doing research for someone else. *You'd* be the writer. *You'd* get the credit. Think of the freedom!"

"Think of us!" I exploded. "Remember us? Your kids? Your twentieth-century city children? I like being spoiled. I like electricity. And telephones. And television and stores. And cars."

"I like Madame Ardelle," Marcia said. "And my school—and libraries. Good, big libraries. Like the ones they have in good, big cities."

"My computer." This was Ben. I didn't like the sound of his voice. He wasn't arguing, he was speculating. "If we had a generator, I could still have my computer, right?"

"Of course."

I looked hopefully at Mom again. There was a gleam in her eye that made me very nervous. "A log cabin," she said quietly. "Ever since I was a kid, I've dreamed of living in a log cabin in the wilderness."

I gulped. It was bad enough when one parent went nuts. When they both did, we were lost! All the ideas our parents had had before seemed sane and comfortable in comparison to this one.

"It's a beautiful dream, Michael," Mom said. I sighed with relief. She'd called it a dream. Like my red BMW, nice but unreal. But then she went on. "A dream worth pursuing."

Dad beamed. "But there's a lot to think about."

"I've *been* thinking," Dad said. "It's possible. It would take planning—and work—but it's possible."

"Okay, then, let's just try it out for a while." Mom nodded. "That's it. From now till September we stay here, just the way we'd planned, helping Minnie Berry with her garden and learning how to get along the way she does. *Brunhilda* can be our homestead for now. We can see how it goes, think about it, find out what the problems would be and the best way to handle them."

"And then what?" Dad asked.

"Then, if we like this life, if we think we can do it, we find ourselves that land and go from there." She poured water through her fingers again. "It *is* beautiful up here. Calm and quiet. No traffic, no sirens, no crowds."

I couldn't stand it. "What about me? I'm going to be a junior! I can't start over in some whole new school up here in the boonies! What about Jason? And Sarah? I have a life, you know! And friendship. And love."

"Human beings are almost infinitely adaptable," Mom said.

"I'll move in with Sarah," I threatened. "Better yet, I'll move in with Jason!"

Mom ignored this. "Your father's right about being spoiled. Over the next few weeks, we'll have to learn to do things in very different ways. Minnie Berry will be a wonderful resource. We'll learn everything we can from her."

"Phooey," Marcia said. Mom ignored this, too.

"I could help build a log cabin," Ben said. "We could do it sort of like Minnie Berry's, only bigger." Now Ben had a gleam in his eye. "And I could catch lots of trout. We could practically live on trout." He picked up the fishing rod he had set down temporarily. "I'd start now, if you guys would get out of the water."

"Miss Berry could teach me to ride her mule," Rick suggested, "and I could be the one who rides to town to get stuff."

"We'll *walk* to town," Dad said. "In fact, we'll do that today. It'll help us start getting in shape for the pioneer life."

"But town is ten miles away!" I protested.

Dad shook his head. "Not that far. More like six. Seven, tops."

"Terrific."

Mom got to her feet. "We'd better get started. There are some things we need from a grocery. And we'll have to let people know where we are and what our plans are."

Plans, I thought. Some plans. A large, buzzing, flying something dive-bombed me, and I stood up, dripping. "I'm going to get the Deep Woods Off." I picked up my shoes and socks.

"I'll go with you," Marcia said.

"Get changed for hiking," Dad said. "We'll buy the stuff we need to turn *Brunhilda* into the Skinner Family Homestead. Think of it, kids, we're about to embark on the greatest adventure of our lives! We're at the beginning of a whole new era!"

"What about lunch?" This, of course, was Rick.

Mom climbed up onto the bank. "We'll pack sandwiches and eat them on the trail to town."

Marcia and I started back to *Brunhilda*. "Meeting adjourned," Dad called after us.

"I suppose they'll expect me to go to some one-room schoolhouse," Marcia grumbled, kicking at the pine needles underfoot. "And take violin lessons from the local band director. If they even have one."

I had far more important concerns. Like Sarah. And Jason. Would Jason still love me if I became a pioneer? And how would we see each other? Philadelphia was hours and hours away. I was about to turn sixteen, of course, but I couldn't even drive down for weekends. There was nothing to drive.

I did not want to live in the wilderness. I did not want to be a pioneer. It was all very well for Ben, who was a complete loner. All he needed was a fishing pole and a generator for his computer. And it was okay for Rick, whose favorite companions were animals, anyway. There were plenty of those up here. And there would be a school for Marcia. Probably one with a real violin teacher. And a library. Give her enough books and she'd manage. But what about me? What about me?

..... Getting in Shape .....

Marcia, already dressed for the hike, was sitting cross-legged on her bed, playing her violin. She says it's a good way to handle stress.

I took a bottle of sunscreen out of an overhead bin and slammed the door—hard. That's a good way, too. "They wouldn't!" I said. "They just wouldn't!"

Marcia took a deep breath and let it out slowly as she drew her bow over the strings. "Don't count on it."

I went outside. Ben and Dad were huddled in conversation behind *Brunhilda,* gesturing toward her from time to time.

Mom was helping Rick with his backpack. "Listen, Mom—" I started.

"Tuck your jeans into your hiking boots," she said, "in case of ticks."

"Ugh!" I shuddered.

"And poison ivy. And snakes."

"Snakes? What kinds of snakes?" My only previous acquaintance with snakes had been with a python named Monty who was with us briefly during Dad's business. I had liked Monty only when he was safely in his cage.

"Well . . ." Mom looked around as if a snake might be lurking nearby, watching and listening. "They're pretty rare, but there might be timber rattlers up here."

24

"Rattlers? Rattlers? You mean with poison?" I stepped away from *Brunhilda*. All those rocks under her had spaces between them. Nooks. Crannies. Perfect places for a rattlesnake to hide.

"Of course with poison," Mom said. "But I told you, they're rare."

"It only takes one," I pointed out.

"Just tuck in your jeans, and you'll be nicely protected."

"Timber rattlers are very shy," Rick said. "They'd sooner run away from people than bite them."

"Where'd you hear that?" I asked.

"I was a Junior Ranger, remember? I read it in a book."

"What if I meet one that hasn't read that book?"

"Don't worry about it," Mom said. "I can practically guarantee we won't meet any timber rattlers."

Practically, she'd said. I wasn't taking any chances. I found a nice, stout stick to take along.

"You can play your violin later," Mom called to Marcia. "We need to get started!"

Marcia played faster, but finished the piece she was playing. For her, that's rebellion.

Buffy, who can always tell when someone's going somewhere, frisked around Rick, tail wagging, actually drooling with anticipation. "You're going, you're going," he assured her. Czar Nicholas, still lying on *Brunhilda*'s dashboard, gazed contentedly through the windshield. I envied him.

Dad and Ben finished their deliberations and joined us. "We've made a list of what we'll need," Dad said. "Everybody wear your packs. We'll have a lot to carry back."

I groaned. Six miles—seven, tops—with full packs. In what felt like ninety-five degrees and one hundred percent humidity. I probably wouldn't even survive till September!

As we were about to start, we heard a familiar chirring sound. The undergrowth moved and Chatter stepped daintily out from under a bush, a long, dark something dangling from her jaws and trailing on either side.

I was through *Brunhilda*'s door, up the three steps, and into the galley by the time Mom called out that it was only a garter snake.

"Only," Rick wailed. "Only! She's killed it!"

With great difficulty Mom persuaded the weeping Rick to postpone the burial service. She had to let him leave the snake's corpse in the refrigerator. Then, to protect the rest of the wildlife of the Adirondack Mountains, she put Chatter inside and locked the door.

If we had to have a homestead in the wilderness, I realized, Chatter could be a real asset.

"We're off!" Dad cried at last, and plunged into the woods toward Minnie Berry's.

The rest of us fell into place behind him. Mom started to whistle and Ben joined her. I let everybody go ahead of me, then walked very carefully, my stick clasped firmly in my right hand—step, *thump*, step, *thump*.

By the time we'd reached Minnie Berry's place, I'd abandoned my snake stick. With everybody else in the family tromping along ahead of me, making all that noise, I figured somebody else would get bitten first. Anyway, the stick kept catching in the undergrowth.

When we came out of the woods, Lucifer—the aging, black, mostly Labrador retriever that Miss Berry claimed was a vicious watchdog—barked once, then struggled to his feet and came to the end of his chain to greet us, tail waving gently. Rick ran over to hug him, and he licked Rick's face from chin to forehead. Ben kept Buffy up among the trees, because Miss Berry had warned us that Lucifer attacked other dogs.

Caliban, the big, tattered black tomcat, emerged from under the sagging porch of the old log cabin and rubbed himself against Rick's knees. But Miss Berry was nowhere to be seen.

"Miss Berry!" Mom called. "Miss Berry!"

"No need to shout; I'm not deaf." The gravelly voice came from behind us, and we turned to see Minnie Berry emerge from the ramshackle building that was the mule's barn. Her hair was pulled back into a bun, but wisps had escaped to frame her face with a white fringe. When I first saw her, I'd been reminded of the dried apple puppets we made in third grade, and I thought of them again. If anything, her face was even more wrinkled than that. She wore a man's undershirt and overalls so faded, it was hard to tell they'd ever been blue. The cuffs were rolled up so that her bony legs showed above the black high-top basketball shoes she wore on her feet. She was using the pitchfork she carried like a cane. She looked us over, taking in our hiking boots and backpacks. "You planning a trip?"

"We're going in to town," Dad explained. "To pick up a few supplies. Is there anything we can get for you?"

Miss Berry squinted into the sun, which was well up over the trees that surrounded her clearing. "Walking, are you?"

Dad nodded. "I thought the hike would be good for us. We've decided to join you."

"Beg pardon?"

"In your pioneering life. We're going to find ourselves a piece of land and build a little homestead."

Miss Berry's eyes widened. "Up here? In the mountains?"

Dad grinned. "Near as we can find a place."

"You wouldn't just want to think about a nice summer cottage. On Lake George, maybe."

"Down there with the tourists?" Dad's voice was horrified. "Never. We want wilderness. That's the whole point."

"And you want to stay the year round, do you?" Dad nodded. The old woman shook her head. "It's no game," she said.

"We know," Mom put in. "So we're just trying it out for now. Getting a feel for it."

"And the first thing we need to do is get in shape. A brisk walk to town and back should help."

Miss Berry leaned on her pitchfork, which dug itself into the ground a little. "That oughta just about do it." She looked toward the sun again. "Getting pretty late in the day. You'd best be off right snappily, or you'll be finding your way back in the dark."

I didn't like the sound of that.

"Of course, it depends on the pace you set," Miss Berry went on, "and how long you spend in town. But it gets dark fast up here once evening comes. Shadows and all. Trees."

"We'll be down and back before you know it," Dad said confidently. "Should we go the way I went when I rode your mule, or is there a better way?"

"Best stick to the road. There's a shortcut, but you'd get lost, sure."

Road. I liked that. It sounded civilized.

Dad nodded. "The road it is. Now, what can we bring you?"

Miss Berry shook her head. "I do my town shopping once a month, and I'm not in the habit of needing things in between." She wiped sweat off her forehead with the back of her hand. "That's something you learn living the pioneering life."

"Okay. Just thought we'd check."

"Best go, now, and get yourselves in shape." She laughed a small, dry laugh. "In shape. Come for supper when you get back—assuming you do." She looked at Rick and winked. "Dessert, too."

Rick grinned. "Gingerbread?" It was Miss Berry's gingerbread that had made Rick decide he liked her in the first place.

"Guess you'll have to wait and see. Go on. Time's a-wasting." With that, she turned and limped back into the barn. Gabriel, the mule, greeted her with a loud hee-haw.

Mom looked at Dad and shrugged her shoulders. "Tough lady."

"Pioneer." Dad cleared his throat and said in his heartiest voice, "All right, Skinners—onward!"

Dad headed off down past the barn, the rest of us trailing along behind. Ben brought Buffy around through the woods to meet us. *Six miles* kept ringing in my head. *Seven, tops.* I had never walked that far in my life, and here I was in jeans and heavy hiking boots under a sun that would send mad dogs and Englishmen scurrying for cover. The canteen on my belt bumped heavily against my leg. At least we had water. And we'd stop for lunch in a while.

Mom started whistling again. Ben and Dad joined in. Rick hummed along. Marcia walked with her head high and her arms swinging at her sides. Okay, I thought, and lifted my chin. I could be as good a Skinner as anyone.

Then we came to what Miss Berry had called "the road." It was two wheel ruts (and I do mean ruts) with grass and weeds growing in the middle. Far from the wide, smooth expanse I'd expected, it was a rocky, narrow track through the trees. At home there are sidewalks wider. "This is a road?" I said to Marcia.

She looked carefully before answering. "Tire tracks," she pointed out. "And oil on the grass in the middle. It's a road, all right. I wonder who uses it."

"Maybe Minnie Berry has a boyfriend." I laughed. "Another pioneer. I'll bet he comes up to visit her every Saturday night."

"Yeah. And for entertainment they churn butter."

We both laughed. Briefly. We soon discovered that walking on this so-called road was no laughing matter. It required all our concentration. We were heading downhill, and rain had washed out great gullies in the ruts. I kept slipping. And turning my ankles. Hiking boots were supposed to prevent this, but mine didn't. The whistling and humming stopped. The air around us seemed to be getting even hotter.

"The only thing good about this road," I told Marcia, twisting my ankle again, "is that it's in the shade." Something bit the back of my neck.

"Bugs like shade, too," Marcia said and slapped her arm.

Soon we were going downhill so sharply that in spite of gullies and rocks, we had a tendency to increase our speed as we went. In a little while Rick and Buffy were actually *running* ahead of the rest of us, while we tried to slow our progress as best we could.

"We're making good time," Dad shouted, in an effort to see this steady acceleration as a good thing.

"Just be careful!"

Mom's warning came too late. Just as she said it, Buffy dodged in front of Rick, who tripped over her and went down. Dad, trying to stop, grabbed for the trunk of a small tree near him, missed, stumbled on Rick's legs and went down next, with Mom on top of him and Marcia on top of her. Ben, who had managed to deflect himself sideways, caught his toe in a gully, and rolled off down the hillside, flattening small bushes as he went. He landed firmly against a huge tree.

Luckily, I was far enough behind to see what was happening. To avoid falling, I just sat and slid into the pileup on my rear. By the time my boots touched Marcia, the tangle of arms and legs that was most of the Skinner family had come to a halt. Buffy, having caused the whole thing, was unscathed. She bounced around us, barking, wanting in on the game.

It took a while for everybody to get untangled and check for concussions and broken bones. Except for scrapes and bruises, we all seemed to be intact. The worst problem was a slight bend in Dad's pack frame.

"I was just about to suggest we take a rest, anyway," Dad said, taking his pack off and leaning it against a tree.

Rick brushed the dirt out of his hair and rubbed his knees. "Let's eat," he said.

Ben crawled up the hill to join us. "Did you see where I stopped? If that tree hadn't been there, I'd have gone over a cliff!"

Mom took off her pack and went to look. She stood very still for a moment, staring down, then turned back with a fixed smile on her face. "It's time for lunch," she said, her voice sounding thin. "Definitely time for lunch."

While she was getting the sandwiches, I went to check out the cliff. It was a sheer rock face, dropping straight down about four stories. I turned around very quickly and hurried back to the road, remembering what Minnie Berry had said about coming back in the dark. "Let's not stop for too long," I said.

We ate our sandwiches hurriedly. Then we brushed ourselves off, put our packs back on, and started walking again. "Stay on the road," Mom warned, "and don't anybody run!"

She didn't have to worry about that for long. Very soon the road started to slope up. And up. And up. Sweat dripped down my forehead and stung my eyes. My feet felt like lead—molten lead. Everybody was breathing hard. Rick was no longer leading. He was now behind me, calling every few minutes for everybody to wait up.

You have to hand it to Dad. He would be a pioneer if it killed him. "We won't—have to—climb—much farther," he'd say. "We'll be out—on the—top—in just a few—more—minutes." Then, after what felt like about an hour, "Not much—farther—now."

Finally the road curved sharply and we really were on top. We came out from under the trees onto a broad, flat meadow dotted with wildflowers. All around us were the blue mounds of other mountain ridges, shimmering in the sun. A breeze rippled the long, golden green grass. It was almost cool.

"This is more like it," Dad said. "This is what life in the mountains is all about! This is the real thing."

I wiped my face with the back of my arm. The hike to get here was what life in the mountains was about, too. Still, I had to admit it was beautiful. There was something about the sunlight that was different from anything I'd ever seen before. Sort of silvery. A hawk flew above us, circling higher and higher.

Mom went to stand next to Dad, and he put his arm around her, backpack and all. They stood together, admiring the view. Marcia had pulled a small paperback out of her pack and was comparing a picture in it to a tiny purple flower. Ben had found a rock and was sitting on it, drinking from his canteen. Buffy, tail wagging, nose to the ground, disappeared into the tall grass.

"Wouldn't it be great to build our cabin right here?" Dad asked.

Mom looked dreamily out at the mountains and the blue sky and nodded. "Perfect."

Dad turned to us. "What do you think, kids. Wouldn't this be great?"

Marcia, now absorbed in the investigation of a large yellow flower, didn't respond. Ben shrugged. I shook my head.

"Where's Rick?" Dad asked.

I glanced around. He wasn't in the meadow with us. "He's probably just back down the road a little way," I said. "He was having trouble keeping up."

"Rick!" Mom shouted. "Rick! Where are you?"

The only sounds were the breeze and the crickets.

"Rick! Richard Skinner! Answer me!"

"Over here!" Rick's voice came faintly from off somewhere to my left. "Blueberries."

"What?" Mom yelled.

"Blueberries!"

We followed the sound of Rick's voice and found him, his chin smeared with blue, cheerfully stuffing berries into his mouth. He was surrounded by thick bushes with small dark leaves. They were covered with berries. Some were still small and green, but most were fat, and dusty blue. There was absolutely no doubt what they were. They looked exactly like the ones in the grocery store. I pulled a couple off and popped them into my mouth. They were warm from the sun and very sweet.

Mom, who had probably planned to scold Rick for putting things into his mouth without checking first with her, didn't say a word. She just picked one and ate it. Then smiled and ate another, and another.

"Looks like Rick found us dessert," she said. "We can come back tomorrow with a bucket."

It wasn't long before all our lips and fingers were blue. These were the best blueberries I'd ever tasted in my whole life. Maybe picking them myself had something to do with it. Maybe knowing that they were just there, all by themselves, and free. Sort of as if God had grown them for us. Whatever it was, I almost began to think Dad was right. It would be great to live up here where a cool breeze always blew, where the sun shone with that funny, silvery light and hawks flew overhead, with the mountains all around and blueberries free for the picking. Maybe homesteading wouldn't be so bad after all.

That's when we heard the noise a little downhill from us. That's when we saw the bushes moving. That's when we saw the bear.

.............Stag............

The bear rose up on his back legs and looked at us. The expression on his face seemed to say that this was his berry patch and he was not fond of sharing. He was black and enormous, and close. Very close. Everybody froze. And the bear just looked.

Suddenly Rick started waving his hands in the air. "Boogah, boogah, boogah!" he yelled at the top of his lungs. The bear, startled, turned toward him.

"Hush," Mom whispered. She moved in Rick's direction as slowly as she could, keeping her eyes on the bear. Dad, on Rick's other side, was doing the same. I felt as if I were in a nightmare—you know, when you want to run, but your legs are too heavy to move.

"Boogah!" Rick shouted again.

Marcia had begun backing away from the blueberries, her hands up as if the bear were holding a gun on us. I began backing, too, wishing we were not in a meadow. Wishing there were something to hide behind. Something big. And strong. The bear didn't move.

Then several things happened all at once. Ben's voice rang out practically in my ear. "Get 'im!" And Buffy streaked past me, barking at the top of her lungs. Dad and Mom closed in on Rick from both sides. Mom grabbed one of his hands, Dad the other, and they turned and ran, away from the berry patch, up across the meadow toward the road, dragging a protesting Rick between them. Marcia went after them.

I was about to run, too, when the bear dropped back down to all fours. Buffy, still barking, was heading right for it. Ben started forward, waving a stick in the air. "Come on, Jenny!" he hollered. "The bear's gonna get Buffy. We've got to scare him off."

Everything was happening so fast, I didn't have time to think. I just went with Ben, waving my arms and stamping my feet as he was doing, yelling, "Boogah, boogah!" right toward the bear. Buffy had stopped when she got close, the fur standing up all down her neck and along her back, barking and snarling as if she were just waiting for an opening to rush in and tear the bear apart. The bear, head down, was swaying back and forth, watching Buffy.

"Boogah, boogah!" Ben and I yelled together as we stamped closer. The bear looked up at us, its nose twitching, then back at Buffy. It growled a low, menacing growl and then, slowly, turned its back and lumbered a few steps away. We stopped. Had we scared it? Buffy barked. The bear looked over its shoulder, then turned and stood up again, as if trying to decide whether we were really crazy enough to keep coming.

With a last "boogah," Ben threw the stick. It sailed over the bear's head and landed in the bushes behind it. With a snort and a snuffle, the bear dropped back to its feet and hurried off down the hill. The last we saw of him was his broad black rump disappearing under the trees. Buffy barked once or twice more, as if to say "and don't come back!" and then bounded back to join us, her tail wagging.

Ben, grinning from ear to ear, brushed his hands in satisfaction. "Guess we took care of him!" he said.

I grinned back at him. "I guess so."

Ben and Buffy started back to where the others were waiting. When I turned to go with them, I noticed my knees. They were shaking so hard I could barely walk. My heart was thudding violently, and it came to me with sudden, awful force. I, Jenny Skinner, had chased a bear. A real, live, huge, furry, black, *wild* bear!

Suddenly I wanted to get off the top of this mountain, out of this beautiful meadow, and into town. In fact, I wanted to go home, to the nice, safe, bearless streets of suburban Philadelphia. Now! I didn't care about silvery sunlight or beautiful mountains or free blueberries. I wanted to go home.

Rick was crying when I finally got back to the road. "But I did the right thing!" he was telling Mom. "Black bears are shy and they hardly ever attack people." This is what he'd said about the snakes. As far as Rick was concerned, apparently, no animal was really dangerous. "It's true! Harvey told me so." (Harvey's a ranger who befriended Rick at a park we stayed in during our getaway.)

Mom, who looked about to cry herself, shook her finger under his nose. "Harvey's a grown-up! Besides, he carries a gun!"

"He wouldn't shoot a bear with it," Rick protested.

"He would if he had to," Mom said. "You are never, never, under any circumstances, to 'boogah' at a bear again, do you hear me, Richard Skinner?"

Rick sniffed and nodded. "He did run away, though."

"This time." Mom turned to Ben and me. "You were very brave. But I want you to promise, too. And Marcia. You are not to chase a bear ever again. Promise!"

"Cross my heart," I said. It was one of the easiest promises I'd ever made. Marcia and Ben nodded.

Dad had said nothing through it all. He was staring off in the direction the bear had gone, frowning. Now he turned to us. "I hadn't thought about something like this when I suggested homesteading," he said.

Good, I thought. He's changed his mind. As usual, I was wrong.

"As confident as I was about this family's ability to make it in the wilderness, I had no real sense of what we could do. Together. As a team. This was our first confrontation and we came through! Even before we'd had a chance to learn how to handle ourselves. Think how we'll be when we've had a little experience!"

Mom handed Rick a tissue. "So far, experience tells me that we need to be more careful around blueberries." She shifted her backpack. "And we don't want to come back through this meadow after dark. So let's get on to town."

I tried not to think about bears and darkness. "How far is town?" Marcia asked. Just what I was wondering.

"Not far," Dad said. "We'll be down to the highway before you know it."

As with many other predictions our father has made, this was something less than accurate. But I'll skip the details and provide only the really important words—heat, bugs, thirst, exhaustion, and *mountains.*

When we did reach the highway, even Buffy had had enough. She was limping, trying to figure out how to walk without actually touching a paw to the ground. I knew how she felt. I could feel blisters on both my heels and on my right little toe.

"Canteen!" Dad groaned, and sank onto a large rock

where the two ruts we'd been following met the pavement of the highway.

"Empty!" Mom said, illustrating her point by holding it upside down. "You finished it half an hour ago, remember? Anybody else have water?"

Nobody did. Buffy had stretched herself out in the shade of the rock, her tongue dragging in the dust.

Mom looked down the highway. "It doesn't matter," she said. "We're there!"

She pointed at a sign next to the road that proclaimed, TOWN OF STAG. I didn't see any town. All I could see was the road, lined on both sides with trees. Nevertheless, we cheered weakly.

Dad didn't join us. He shook his head. "We're not there yet," he said.

"What do you mean?" Mom asked. "The sign's right there."

"That's the Town. We're going to the Village."

"What's the difference?" Marcia asked.

"A technical difference," Dad said. "As far as I can tell, a town up here is just some lines on a map, not a town in the sense of actual people and businesses and buildings. Those are in the village."

"And where is the village?" Mom asked.

"Over that little rise."

I looked in the direction he was pointing. Little rise? The road went steadily upward toward the sky.

"I'm not going any farther," Rick said. He shucked off his backpack and sat down in the sand next to the highway. "Me and Buffy'll wait here."

"Buffy and I," Mom corrected him.

"Okay, you, too," he said.

"Nobody is staying here." Dad's voice was firm. "The Skinner family is getting in shape. We are in this together, and we will meet the obstacles together. The pioneers did not sit down and refuse to go any farther." He started to struggle up from his rock.

"Sit," Mom said to Dad, as if he were Buffy. She unbuckled her frame pack and slipped it off. "We're all going on. It's just that we need a break." She smiled her tough, brave smile. "The rest of the way will be easy, now that we've got pavement to walk on. Smooth and straight and even."

"I'm staying here," Rick repeated.

"Then you'll miss the ice-cream cones," Mom said.

"Ice-cream cones?"

"Two scoops each."

"Okay," Rick said grudgingly. "But I get to have sprinkles on mine."

"Are we going to have to walk to town every time we need anything?" practical Marcia asked. "Forever?"

Dad looked off up the road and didn't answer. Marcia turned to Mom, who had become engrossed in the progress of an ant across the top of the rock she and Dad were sitting on. The only sound was the rustling of leaves in the birch trees along the road.

When we started walking again, the question was still unanswered.

Somehow, we all made it to the other sign, the one that said, VILLAGE OF STAG. For something so painful to get to, Stag wasn't much. Just a few blocks of business district and a couple of streets of houses. But we didn't care. We were there. And it had everything we needed.

There was a grocery store, a post office, a bank, a hardware store. All the basics. Except, as Rick pointed out, an ice-cream store. There was, however, a drugstore with a picture of an ice-cream cone in the window. Even though it was late—after four o'clock—and the shadows of the buildings were already stretching across the street, we went inside. Mom had promised.

While we sat on the red plastic-covered stools, eating our ice cream and savoring the movement of the air created by the ceiling fan, we planned our assault on the Village of Stag. Time was of the essence. Ben and Dad would go to the hardware store, while Mom went to the grocery. My assignment was the post office. Marcia wanted to find the local library and get some materials on wilderness living. Rick, who had gone outside to share his cone with Buffy, would stay with her and dog-sit.

I finished my chore first. I'd sent postcards to everybody who needed to know where we were, assuring Jason of my undying love and telling Sarah of my parents' descent into madness. As I headed back to the drugstore, I saw a sign with an arrow pointing off to STAG LAKE BEACH. I stood for a moment, looking at it. If we were going to stay here, I needed to find out if there were kids around. Where better to do that than the beach? Where else would teenagers be on the hottest July day in living memory?

It wasn't far. I passed several houses and heard rock music. Half a block farther and I could see the blue expanse of the lake, surrounded by tree-covered hills. I stopped under a tree to check out the beach.

It was the local hangout, all right. A Frisbee was being tossed around kind of haphazardly, but very little else was going on. Two couples were sitting together on blankets, sort of nuzzling each other. Everybody else was either lying in the sun or just standing around. There were several radios, all tuned to the same rock station.

Although it was still plenty hot, and the water looked awfully inviting, none of the older kids were swimming. There was a section marked off with white rope and plastic markers, but only a few little kids were actually in the water. They had the right idea. More than anything, I wanted to get into that lake. I left the shelter of the tree and started toward the beach, remembering too late the way I looked. I'd have turned back, but a few of the closer kids had seen me.

"Hey, lookit here!" somebody shouted. "A real, live, genuine hiker. Hey, hiker!"

"Oooh, look at those fancy new boots," someone else said.

"Kinda hot for mountain climbing, don'cha think?"

I glanced down at myself and wished I could disappear. Great heavy, orange hiking boots, sweat-soaked T-shirt, damp jeans. No makeup. I couldn't even imagine what my hair looked like! I turned around as fast as I could and headed back to Main Street. And Dad wanted me to actually go to school with these kids? I'd sooner face another bear!

When I joined Rick and Buffy in front of the drugstore, I felt awful. Here I was, mere weeks away from my sixteenth birthday, utterly wheelless, boyless, friendless, alone, and bereft. And facing a seven-mile hike upward through bear country before I could even go back to sleep to dream about home and friends and that red BMW.

Marcia arrived shortly after I did, her backpack bulging with books. "I found tons of great stuff," she said, dumping her pack on the curb. "This library's teeny—in a regular house—but there's an arrangement that lets them get any book from any other library in the whole state. Besides,

they have this really great collection about the plants and animals of the Adirondacks. Also gardening." She was rummaging through the pack. "Here's one called *Homesteading*. Isn't that great? And one about building log cabins." Marcia had joined the enemy!

"How're you going to carry all those books back?" Rick asked, very sensibly, I thought.

"You could take a couple for me," she suggested, taking some out of her pack. She handed me one. "You, too."

Before I even had time to protest, Mom appeared, carrying two stuffed grocery bags. "No way, Marcia. Everybody has to take some of these. If we pack carefully, I think we can manage. Shopping was terrible. If I got something big enough to last, it would be too big to carry. So I had to get small sizes, and we'll just have to come back a lot."

Just then, Ben came out of the hardware store. At least we assumed it was Ben. What it looked like was an enormous animated roll of corrugated black plastic pipe walking on blue-jeaned, hiking-booted legs.

"What is that? How are we going to carry that?" Mom asked.

"This is the pipe to do *Brunhilda*'s plumbing," he said. "I've got more stuff inside."

He put the pipe down on the sidewalk and went back into the store. I looked at Mom. She looked at me. And Marcia. And Rick. Maybe, I thought, we could make a backpack that would fit Buffy.

"Where's your father?" Mom asked Ben when he came back carrying a bulging bag and a shiny new shovel.

"He went to that garage—Henry's—to get some gas for the generator. I thought he'd be back by now."

A pickup truck full of teenage kids came down the street.

I ducked behind Marcia's book. I couldn't face any more of them.

As I was peeking out from behind the book to make sure they were safely past, an open Jeep came along and I caught just a glimpse of the driver—possibly the most gorgeous male human being I had ever seen. Sandy hair, enormous shoulders, khaki shirt with sleeves rolled up over major muscles, an incredible tan. I ducked back behind the book, pretending intense interest in *Reptiles of the Northeastern United States.* As soon as he'd gone by, I looked again. Astounding!

Marcia shook her head. "Too old," she said.

"Mind your own business." The Village of Stag had undergone a transformation in my mind. A good place, it was. Well worth a small hike.

Dad didn't come and didn't come. Mom's eyes got that tight look around them, and the shadows on the street got longer and longer. I thought again about bears in the darkness. And cliffs. Marcia sat on the curb and read one of her books. Rick wandered back into the drugstore. I watched the shadows grow.

Suddenly, off down the street, we heard what sounded like a gunshot. Then another. Could there be terrorists in a place like Stag? I thought wildly.

"Backfire," Ben said. "Nothing to worry about."

Rick came running out of the drugstore and Marcia looked up from her book, so we all saw the ancient truck that turned onto Main Street two blocks away. Even from there the roar of its engine was enough to hurt the ears. There was a grinding sound as it changed gears. It looked as if it could be the oldest truck in the state of New York. Its hood was long and almost pointed, and there were bulbous fenders on each side, with huge, round headlights riding on them like the eyes of an insect. The cab was partly dark green, partly rust colored. The door on the side toward us was a dull red. In the back its sides weren't metal, like a pickup truck, but wooden, like a fence.

It roared toward us. Then it began to slow down. It backfired again, the noise echoing off the buildings. People began collecting on the street to look. With a squeal of metal on metal, it stopped directly in front of us, and the driver leaned toward the window. It was Dad.

"Load 'em up, move 'em out!" he shouted.

I glanced around. Nobody here knows us, I told myself. Nobody.

Leaving the engine on—quieted now to a dull, hiccuping growl—Dad slid across the seat and jumped out. "The other door's wired shut," he explained. "What are you waiting for? Get that stuff in the back, and let's get on the road. It's getting late."

Nobody said a word. As soon as Dad had lifted out the piece of fence that formed the back of the truck, we piled everything in. "Ellie, you ride up front with me, kids and Buffy in the back."

And so, roaring and backfiring, growling and grinding, we left Stag. I kept Marcia's book about reptiles firmly in front of my face.

...Basic Transportation...

Besides avoiding bears and cliffs, there were two theoretical advantages to going back in the truck. One was that we wouldn't have to force our tired bodies and blistered feet to walk all those miles. The other was that we'd get back much faster by vehicle than by foot, and wouldn't have to worry so much about traveling in the dark.

These advantages remained theoretical. Oh, the first part of the trip was okay—the part where Dad was driving along the highway at the breakneck speed of about thirty miles an hour, which seemed as fast as the decrepit old truck could move. The sun was still hot, so the wind in our faces felt good, and we were sitting down—all except for Buffy, who insisted on standing with her nose out between the wooden slats, her eyes closed, and the wind blowing her ears back.

Then Dad turned onto the dirt road. The old truck backfired, bucked, squealed, bounced into the ruts, and came to a sudden stop. There was an unmistakable sound of breaking glass from the general direction of the grocery bags. Ben, who'd been sitting at the back, actually rose into the air and then returned rather violently to the wooden truck bed. Buffy went down, taking Rick, who'd been holding her collar, with her. Marcia had been hanging on to one of the uprights from the moment she'd climbed in, so she just got a stiff jolt. I cracked my elbows and head on the cab behind me. The roar of the engine stopped abruptly, and we were surrounded by silence.

"You forgot to put in the clutch, Michael," Mom said, her voice loud and clear.

There was a long moment before Dad answered. "I was putting in the clutch, dear," he said, "when the pedal broke off."

There was another long moment. I looked through the cab window. Mom had one hand over her mouth and was looking intently out her window.

"Everybody out!" Dad yelled.

The delay wasn't as long as it could have been. By the time we'd tied the cargo down with the rope Mom kept in her pack, Dad had discovered that the clutch could be worked—carefully—without its pedal. He started the engine again, and we clambered back in. Buffy rode in the cab with Mom and Dad this time, since we couldn't persuade her to lie down and Rick was sure she'd be hurt. Unfortunately, there wasn't room in the cab for the rest of us, so we had to take our chances.

If the ruts that passed for a road were hard to walk on, they were almost impossible to drive on. The truck, which Ben named Quasimodo (the main character in *The Hunchback of Notre Dame*, a name that stands for *ugly*), as we roared and jolted along, seemed to have no shock absorbers—no suspension system of any kind. We felt every ridge and gully and rock. It was impossible to maintain constant contact between our bottoms and the truck bed. What we needed back there was a mattress. Lots of mattresses.

Once, when we bounced into a particularly deep hole, the back bumper fell completely off. Ben alerted Dad to the loss by pounding on the window, and we stopped long enough for Ben to load the bumper into the truck with us. "It was only wired on!" he yelled.

"All the easier to fix," Dad yelled back.

Now Mom's hands completely covered her face. She was shaking her head.

While we were stopped, the sun sank behind the mountains, and we found ourselves in deep shadow. Mosquitoes and other biting, flying things came out and landed on any bit of exposed skin they could find, and the heat that had been making life miserable all day disappeared. Suddenly, mysteriously, and completely. As if someone had flipped a switch.

With a roar and a lurch, we started on again, the back tires spinning for a moment before getting a bite on the dirt. As long as we kept moving at a decent rate, the bugs weren't too bad. But if we slowed down, they descended. Unfortunately, we were seldom moving at a decent rate. Whenever the road sloped upward—which it did a good part of the time—Quasimodo seemed to lose heart. It got slower and slower, till Dad had it in first gear, and then it didn't seem to be able to force itself over five miles an hour.

Also, whenever we were going uphill, we kids had to hold on to the ropes that tied the cargo in place so that we wouldn't slide down and out the back. We sprayed ourselves all over with Off, but though that cut down on the biting, the bugs still came and buzzed their high, nasty, whining buzz in our ears. We couldn't slap them away because we were holding on to the ropes with both hands.

When the road sloped down, the truck went faster, and the bugs got blown away, but it wasn't much more comfortable. For one thing, the wind that blew the bugs away also blew on us, and it wasn't warm. Besides, going down, we got crammed against the cab with all the cargo. Then, when we hit bumps, we were likely to bounce into one another. Bone to bone.

As it got darker, it got colder. I could feel Marcia shivering next to me, and for some reason, her shivering made me start to shiver, too. Pretty soon the four of us were huddled together, shaking and chattering. Maybe it was having sweated so hard all day that made us so cold now.

By the time we arrived at Minnie Berry's, it was almost completely dark, and Dad had discovered that the truck's headlights didn't work. Neither did the taillights.

When Quasimodo screeched and shuddered to a stop in front of the old log cabin, Lucifer hurried to the end of his chain and stood barking at us. You could hardly blame him. He'd probably never seen or heard anything like Quasimodo before. Buffy, leaning past Mom, barked back. Vicious Lucifer stopped barking and retreated under the porch.

Dad cut the engine, and I discovered that its roar had gotten into my brain. I kept on hearing it, like the sound of the surf in a seashell. Aching all over, I climbed out. The ground seemed to be vibrating under my feet.

Minnie Berry came out onto her porch.

"Thought Henry'd junked that thing twenty years ago," she said. "Come in. Stew's waiting."

With a little crowding, we could all fit around the old oak table in the cabin's main room. It was already set with Miss Berry's blue enameled plates and dark blue glasses. There was a bowl of floating hollyhock blossoms in the center.

The orangey light from the kerosene lamp overhead cast flickering shadows as Miss Berry limped back and forth, putting the food onto the table. Mom offered to help. "You just stay where you are. I reckon you're in need of a place to sit that won't try to throw you off." Mom didn't argue. Dad was staring down at his plate, his face grim. Nobody said much after that. We just ate. The fire in the wood stove crackled comfortingly behind us.

When the stew and biscuits were all gone, Miss Berry took a pan out of the warming oven and set it directly in front of Rick's plate. "'Tisn't gingerbread," she told him. "But I daresay you'll be able to choke it down."

It was a cobbler, made with fresh raspberries. "Picked them this afternoon," she said, and plunked down a pitcher of milk. "Crop's almost done for this year."

The first bite of raspberry cobbler made me almost forget the tribulations of the day. It was delicious! Rick spooned up mouthful after mouthful, scarcely stopping to breathe. Ben was sitting up a little straighter. Mom smiled. Even Dad seemed to perk up a bit.

"We saw a bear," Rick said around a mouthful.

"Old Bruno, that'd be. Up by the blueberry patch?"

"Yep. Buffy scared it away."

I was about to remind him of Ben's and my part in the affair, when Miss Berry chuckled. "A mouse could scare Bruno away. He's an old fella. Friend of mine, you might say."

We all concentrated on our dessert.

"So," Miss Berry said to Dad, settling back into her chair, "you've got yourself a truck. What'd Henry take you for?"

Dad swallowed a bite of cobbler and attempted a smile.

"We worked out a suitable deal, I believe."

"That much, eh?" Miss Berry turned to Mom. "Henry's old granddaddy Joe used to have a livery stable down in Stag."

"A horse trader?" Mom said.

"Right. It's in the blood, you might say. Did you buy or lease?" This last was back to Dad.

"Lease. It's purely a temporary expedient."

"I'm sure it is," she said.

"All I was after was basic transportation."

"You got it," Mom said dryly.

Dad frowned as he scraped the last bit of raspberry from his dish. Then he straightened his shoulders. "Well"—his voice took on a bit of its old enthusiasm—"it's been a day of learning. Anything new takes a little getting used to. But now that we have our supplies, we can settle in and get on with our new life." He clapped Ben on the shoulder. "Ben and I will plumb *Brunhilda* tomorrow, and you others can get started in the garden."

I sighed. My body was going to need to recuperate for a while. A day at least. Maybe a week.

Miss Berry glanced over at me. "Not much needed tomorrow," she said. "A little weeding. A little hoeing."

Oh, well, I thought. A little weeding and a little hoeing. And four of us to do it. Not so bad.

"And a few beans to can."

No problem.

"Looks like we've lost the young one," Miss Berry observed.

Rick, his lips stained with raspberries, had fallen asleep with his head on the table beside his empty plate.

"The two of you had better take him on back and put

him to bed. The girls will clean up here. Young Ben can fill the wood box for me, then walk back with the girls."

Dad stood up. "The truck's lights aren't working, so we won't be able to get down the road."

"Eleanor, you take a lantern and walk back," Miss Berry said. "Daniel Boone, here, can follow you in the truck. You won't hurt that old thing going overland."

Dad carried Rick outside, Mom took the lantern, and a few minutes later Quasimodo roared to life, backfired a couple of times, and gradually faded off.

Under Miss Berry's direction, Marcia and I did the dishes and put them away while Ben chopped wood. We were all so tired, we didn't even have the energy to be grumpy about the work. We just did it. Finally we were finished. Miss Berry gave us another lantern and we went outside to collect Buffy.

We found her under the porch curled up against Lucifer's side, both of them sound asleep. Ben whistled, and Buffy scrambled up, her tail wagging. Lucifer opened one eye, made a sort of whuffling sound, and went back to sleep.

Minnie Berry shook her head. "What's the world coming to?"

We said good-night and stumbled off down the path, the lantern making a small pool of light in a huge, cold, terrifying darkness. I was glad Buffy was with us. I wasn't feeling much like a pioneer. "Boogah," I whispered, in case anything was out there among the trees.

At last *Brunhilda* appeared, surrounded by a warm and cozy glow. Her generator was running—a civilized, comforting sound—and light poured from all her windows. With our last shred of energy, we reached the door. Mom opened it. We were home.

.... Homesteading 101 ....

I was standing on the curb outside our house. The red BMW was coming toward me, driven by the gorgeous guy I'd seen in the Jeep. I knew what was going to happen. He was going to pull into the driveway, I was going to get in, and we were going to ride blissfully away into the sunset, his strong right arm around me, my head on his shoulder.

The car came closer. It slowed. It turned in. I reached for the door handle and saw Sarah, my best friend, sitting next to the gorgeous guy. His right arm was around her, and she was smiling. "Hi, Jenny," she said. "How do you like my new car?" I opened my eyes.

"It's about time," Marcia said. "I thought you were going to sleep all day."

I blinked. "What time is it?"

"Nine."

I rubbed my eyes and sat up. The sun was beating down on *Brunhilda,* and our room was hot. Czar Nicholas was stretched out against the wall, as far from my sweaty body as he could get without actually abandoning my bed. "Nine? What's with Dad? What happened to 'rise and shine' and 'up and at 'em'? What happened to pioneers rising with the sun? I thought this was the day we started learning to homestead."

"He's still sleeping—like a rock. He didn't even wake up

53

when Rick jumped down off his bunk and landed on Buffy's tail. I think he overdid the pioneer stuff yesterday."

Marcia was sitting cross-legged on her bed, surrounded by books. I asked, "What are you doing? Studying for the exam?"

"We're going to start working on Miss Berry's garden today, and I want to know everything I can."

"Why? She'll tell us what to do."

Marcia screwed up her face. "Exactly. But I want to know *before* she tells us. In fact, I want to know *better* than she tells us."

"Better? How can you know better than somebody who's been raising vegetables up here for seventy years?"

Marcia sighed one of her patient sighs. "Jenny, just because she's done something for seventy years doesn't mean she's doing it right. She's probably using all sorts of old-fashioned, unscientific methods that cut down on her yield and make her work harder." She held up the book she was reading. "This tells about all the advances in fertilizer and pesticides that have revolutionized farming."

"She's not farming," I said, "and American agriculture does not depend on her yield. She's an old lady growing enough vegetables to get her through the winter."

Marcia didn't answer. She just went back to her reading.

"Do you suppose she grows mushrooms?" I asked. "I haven't had a single one all summer, and they're the only vegetable I really, really like."

Marcia looked up and shook her head at my ignorance. "Mushrooms aren't vegetables, Jenny, they're fungus. *Fungi.* And they don't grow in gardens."

"I didn't think they did," I said. "I just thought she might be growing them in a cellar somewhere or something."

"I doubt it. Too bad we can't go hunting for them in the woods, though."

"Why can't we? Don't they grow up here?"

"Mom won't let us. She says there are too many poisonous ones."

"Maybe we can get some at the grocery next time we go. Now that I've thought about mushrooms, I'm not going to be able to get them out of my mind."

"I doubt that Mom would consider them homesteading necessities, Jenny."

She was probably right. I sighed and dug under my bottom sheet, where I kept the clothes that didn't fit into *Brunhilda*'s tiny closets and drawers. I pulled out a pair of shorts. Wrinkled, but clean. "What's everybody else doing?"

"Ben took Buffy and went fishing. I think he got up at dawn. He left a note."

I nodded. I'd go fishing at dawn, too, if my day was supposed to be spent digging a giant latrine in the woods so we could empty *Brunhilda*'s waste tanks. "I wonder if he'll come back."

"Who knows? Rick's out burying the refrigerated garter snake and the four unidentified body parts Chatter left on the step during the night."

"We should turn that cat loose up near the blueberries. She'd be more than a match for old Bruno." I pictured the scene in the meadow again and started to giggle. All of us frozen with terror and Rick waving his arms like a crazy person. "Boogah, boogah!" I said.

Czar Nicholas jumped off the bed.

"Worked on him, too. Where's Mom?"

"She's outside with the typewriter, writing her next column for the newspaper."

"What about?"

"Homesteading. What else?" Marcia slammed shut the book she was reading. "I don't know why they think we can learn so much from Minnie Berry. She never even went to college."

"You don't need a degree for homesteading," I said, pulling a clean T-shirt over my head. "Anyway, she taught school for sixty years or something."

"She'd never be allowed to teach now. She probably doesn't even have a certificate."

I slipped my feet into my sandals—my blisters couldn't face shoes this morning. "What is your problem with her, anyway?"

"Don't you remember what she said practically the minute she met me? She said I was rude!"

"Well, you were."

"*I* was rude? What do you call holding a gun on a family of innocent tourists?"

"We scared her. Anyway, it wasn't loaded. Her bark's worse than her bite, Marcia."

Marcia flipped her book open again. "Yeah, well it's rude to bark. And just because she's old doesn't mean she knows everything."

"She knows how to make terrific raspberry cobbler!" I said, and headed for the bathroom.

While I was in the galley having a piece of toast with peanut butter on it for breakfast, Dad woke up. He sat up and untangled himself from his sheets and scratched at the beard stubble on his face. (He's had his handlebar mustache for ages, but he quit shaving his beard when *Brun-*

hilda broke down, and it was getting noticeable—scruffy and noticeable.)

"Where is everybody?"

I shrugged. "Out, mostly."

Dad groaned and checked his watch. "Nine-fifteen? How'd it get to be nine-fifteen?" He struggled up from the sofa bed and squeezed past me on his way to the bathroom. "Why didn't somebody wake me? Half the day's gone!"

"Rise and shine!" I said. "Up and at 'em."

Rick came banging up the steps and into the living room. "Come see the snake's grave, Jenny. It's beautiful."

"Beautiful?"

"It is. Come see."

So I followed him into the woods to a little cleared space in the shelter of a huge outcropping of rock. He was right. The grave really was beautiful. He'd outlined an oval with some of the smooth skipping stones he'd gathered the day before (Was it really only yesterday? I thought. It felt as if we'd been here for weeks), and he'd transplanted some moss that looked like stars onto the mound of the grave itself. As usual, he'd made a cross out of two sticks, held together with grass stems, with some tiny blue flowers tied in. Shafts of sunlight penetrated the canopy of pine needles above us and fell in patches on the moss.

There was another, smaller cross, up against the rock, one small stone in front of it. "What's that?"

Rick shrugged. "The other stuff."

I remembered Marcia mentioning miscellaneous body parts. No way to know what animal they represented. Or animals. "You'd better clear away some of the leaves and stones and stuff around here," I said.

"Why? I wanted it to look natural, so the snake would feel at home."

"Unless you're going to lock Chatter into her cat carrier for the rest of the summer, this grave is going to turn into a whole cemetery." I looked up into the branches overhead. "You could call it Forest Lawn."

Rick's face bunched up as if he were going to cry, and I was sorry for making a joke. He felt personally guilty about Chatter's blood lust. As if he'd been killing the animals himself. "Listen, Rick, animals kill other animals. That's the way it is."

"It shouldn't be," he said, and kicked at his pile of skipping stones. "Czar Nicholas doesn't kill things."

"Hey, you're going to have to get used to this, if we're going to spend the rest of our lives in the wilderness." I remembered what Dad had said about hunting. Imagine putting venison on the table in front of Rick!

For once I was glad to hear Dad, his enthusiastic voice in place again, calling for us.

He had on his hiking boots and was holding one of the shovels he'd bought at the hardware store. The roll of plumbing pipe was on the ground next to Quasimodo. "We burn daylight," he said. "Time to get to work."

Mom had put away the typewriter and was looking almost as enthusiastic as Dad. "Rick and Marcia and Jenny, we'll work with Miss Berry. When Ben gets back, of course, he'll help your father."

"And the sooner you begin, the sooner you'll be done!" Dad said.

On our way to Minnie Berry's, as I was keeping an eye out for timber rattlers, I became aware of something moving out in the woods. It was too small to be a bear, too large to be a timber rattler, and it seemed to be following us. In spite of the heat, I could feel goose bumps rising on my arms. I stopped and listened. Rustle, rustle, among the leaves. What could it be? Porcupine? Skunk? And why was it following us? I was just about to say something to Mom, who was leading the way, when I caught a glimpse of a tan tail with a black tip. It was Chatter. I was just as glad she was with us. It was sort of like having a police escort. I felt safer.

"Slept in, did you?" was Miss Berry's greeting when we came out of the woods. She was sitting in a chair on her front porch with a huge bowl on her lap and a basket on the floor next to her.

Mom looked sheepish. "I guess we tired ourselves out yesterday." She didn't mention that she'd written a newspaper column already. "Anyway, here we are, ready to go. What would you like us to do?"

"Depends." Miss Berry put the bowl down and pulled herself to her feet with the help of the porch railing. It wobbled as she stood up, shaking the morning glories that grew across it and up the post to the roof. "I already picked beans, so that's done. But there's garden work and kitchen work and Gabriel's barn."

Rick, who was getting his face-wash greeting from Lucifer, jumped up. "I'll do Gabriel!"

Marcia, having boned up on veggies all morning, naturally chose garden work. So did Mom. I was already sweating, and the sun seemed to be getting hotter by the minute, so I voted for kitchen work, assuming it would be cooler. That just shows how much I had to learn.

Leaning on her hoe as she walked, Miss Berry took us down to the garden to show Mom and Marcia what she wanted them to do. The garden was lots bigger than I'd expected. In fact, I don't know just what I expected—something like the little gardens people had in their backyards at home. A few tomato plants, some beans and cucumbers and peppers, maybe. Minnie Berry's garden was like a whole enormous field. I don't know what an acre looks like, but this had to be at least an acre. Maybe more. It was planted in sections, and there were flowers in it, too. Marigolds and petunias all over the place. One enormous section was corn, already almost shoulder high. I looked at the garden, then at Minnie Berry, as she limped along the rows, telling Marcia and Mom what she wanted. How had she planted it in the first place? How had she managed up till now?

She was growing almost everything. Turnips and potatoes and peas and cabbage and carrots. Along two edges, where the garden came closest to the woods, she had raspberry and currant and blueberry bushes. There was a fence about seven feet high between those and the woods, with strands of barbed wire only a few inches apart. "Discourages freeloaders," she explained. "Like our friend Bruno."

Leaving Mom and Marcia at work, Miss Berry took Rick and me back to the barn. Gabriel hee-hawed in greeting and kicked at the wall. "I don't know," she said, and squinted hard at Rick. "Gabriel's no marshmallow. Maybe you won't be able to handle him."

Rick drew himself up to look as tall as he could. "I'm good with animals."

"He really is," I said.

She frowned, but I thought I caught a twinkle in her eyes. "All right, then, we'll try you out. Go inside and get him first. He has a halter on. Talk quietly to him as you go in, and stay on his left side." She squinted at him. "You do know which is left?"

"Of course!"

"Just checking. Wouldn't hurt to put a hand on him when you go in. Lets him know just where you are. After you've brought him out and tied him to the rail, you'll muck out his stall." She pointed to the pitchfork leaning against the barn. "Old straw goes into the wheelbarrow so you can take it to the manure pile. Put fresh straw down. When you're done, he needs some exercise. You know how to ride?"

"I want to learn!"

Miss Berry nodded. "We'll see how the two of you get along. A mule's a mule. And remember, there's a fine line between courage and foolishness. Gabriel will know if you step over it." She patted Rick's head with a gnarled hand. "Come along, Jennifer."

I followed the old woman up the porch steps. She muttered something about how long it took to tell people what to do and how to do it. "Easier to do it myself," she said.

"Quicker maybe," I said. "Not easier."

She turned on me, and I had an impulse to duck. She narrowed her eyes at me. "Reckon you're right. Bring the beans."

........Green Beans........

Have you ever canned green beans? In the middle of a heat wave over a wood stove? If not, I have one bit of advice for you. Don't. Just don't.

It was easy to see how Minnie Berry could live through an Adirondack winter. Her cabin's small and her wood stove, going full blast, could heat a football stadium.

There aren't any handy knobs and dials on wood stoves that let you turn the heat to low or medium or high, but you can do it, anyway. You control the temperature partly by the size of the fire you make, partly by the kind of wood you use. Miss Berry explained all this to me, as she kept stuffing more wood in, even though it already felt hot enough in the cabin to roast an ox. Or us.

Then there was the humidity. Picture this big iron stove, practically glowing, with four pots on it, each holding gallons and gallons of boiling water. What else do you see in this picture? Steam. Clouds of steam rising over the pots. Well, I'd been warm enough when we first went inside. In half an hour I was soaked. I might as well have been taking a shower. My hair was all stuck to my face, and I could feel positive rivers running down my back and under my arms. Gross!

Canning is very complicated. You have to wash and rinse

the glass jars and set them upside down on towels, and then you have to boil the beans for five minutes to precook them. Then you have to ladle them into the jars, along with some of the boiling liquid, screw the jar lids down almost tight, with these rubber rings in place, and put the full jars in a pot with enough boiling water to completely cover them. You keep the water boiling for twenty-five minutes, then you take the jars out, tighten the lids, and you're done. The process is called "hot pack." For obvious reasons.

You have to be really careful to do it exactly right, or bacteria could grow in the jars, and whoever eats the beans later could get food poisoning and maybe die. This makes canning not only an uncomfortable activity, but a terrifying one. Someone's life could depend on your doing it right. If we were homesteading, I thought, wiping the sweat out of my eyes with the hem of my apron, it would be *our* lives depending on it!

Because everything's hot all the time, you have to handle stuff with tongs, which takes some getting used to. I broke a jar practically first thing when it slipped out of the tongs. Miss Berry didn't say a word, though. She just tightened her lips into a straight line and handed me the broom and dustpan to clean up. I got better at it eventually, but lifting those hot jars out of the pot is very nerve-racking.

After a while we got a break because we'd done all the beans Miss Berry had already snapped. Then we got to sit out on the porch and snap the rest—a basketful that looked as if it would feed the army of a medium-size country. Actually, besides being able to do it out on the porch where there was at least a little breeze and where Caliban came and curled up by my feet, snapping beans is sort of fun.

There's something satisfying in the sound and the feel as you snap them. Something fresh and crisp and green. I don't mean you want to pay somebody to let you do it or anything, just that it's a lot more fun than canning.

"How often do you have to do this?" I asked.

"Canning beans or just canning?"

"Either. Both."

"Beans every day from when they start to ripen until they're done. Canning most days all summer. Peas are nearly over now, then come tomatoes and carrots and beets. Cabbage, onions, greens. And pickling. And fruit. Some canning, some jellies and jams."

I shook my head. "That's a lot of work."

Miss Berry nodded and went on snapping.

"You have to pick them, too."

"Plant, weed, feed, pick, and put up. Like I said, it isn't a game. Summer's a busy time."

I wiped the sweat off my forehead for about the millionth time. "And hot!"

She snapped a particularly long bean into four pieces. She was sweating, too, but it didn't seem to bother her. "Heat's bad this year. Just wait till winter, though. You'll wish you had it back."

Winter. Homesteading in the winter. I refused to think about it.

Rick finished with Gabriel's stall and joined us on the porch. Miss Berry sent him inside to wash his hands and get a pitcher of lemonade out of her refrigerator. Hers is bigger than the one in *Brunhilda* but works the same way, on propane gas instead of electricity.

We each had a glass, and she sent him to take some to

Mom and Marcia in the garden. "Tell them to come up for a bite of lunch when they're ready," she called after him.

"You shouldn't fix us lunch," I said.

"I have no intention of fixing it," she answered, snapping the last of the beans.

When Rick got back, Miss Berry said he could ride Gabriel when we'd finished canning. He came inside with us, and while we sweated through the whole ghastly thing all over again—hot jars and hot beans and steam—he sat in Miss Berry's rocking chair and she told stories.

It was weird, the difference between Miss Berry with anybody else and Miss Berry with Rick. First of all, she talked a lot more. And when she talked, her voice seemed different. Not so gravelly and hard. She told about the way it was when she first started teaching up here, when the only way to get to the school in winter was on skis. She'd had to get there while it was still dark to light a fire in the wood stove so the room would be warm enough when the kids got there. Even so, the ones who sat farthest away sometimes had to keep their coats on all day. It must not have been as good a wood stove as this one, I thought, as sweat dripped off the end of my nose.

The fathers of the students cut the wood they needed back then, and piled it outside the school, but sometimes it would be frozen solid in the morning, and she'd have to use an axe to break it loose. Then the fire would be so hard to start, she'd have to use some of the kerosene from the lamps, sort of like charcoal starter. She told about the bucket and dipper they had for drinking water—no fountains in the hall. (No hall, since it was a one-room school.) The water would be frozen when she arrived, and she'd have to thaw it out on the stove. When they ran out of water, one of the kids would get a bucketful of snow to melt.

"Of course, you couldn't do that anymore," she said, tightening the lid on a jar of beans. "Snow and rain are both poisonous these days."

That reminded her of the snow ice cream they'd made as a treat when the kids had been particularly good, and how she'd let them out in the early spring sometimes for "sugaring," when they collected sap and made maple syrup. They'd pour the boiling syrup on snow and it would harden into candy. I'd heard about this somewhere, and I'd tried it once, but it hadn't worked. The syrup had just melted the snow and the whole thing turned into this runny brown mess. I told Miss Berry about it.

"You were probably using that stuff they call syrup now," she said. "All full of chemicals."

"Yeah, and poisonous snow," Rick said. Miss Berry laughed. For just a moment, I could almost imagine her younger, eighteen or nineteen, with all her students around her, easy with them the way she was with Rick. Then she saw the jar I'd just filled.

"Jennifer Skinner," she said in a voice that could cut glass. "Have I not made it clear that the jars are not to be filled to the top? Do you want them to explode?"

While we were boiling the last jars of beans, Mom and Marcia knocked on the screen door. I couldn't tell if they were just hot, or if they were sunburned, but even through the screen, I could see how red their faces were. And how dirty. They looked even worse than I felt.

"Have a seat on the porch," Miss Berry called to them. "You won't want to come inside just now—it's too hot."

She peered out at them. "There's a pump by the barn. You can wash up there. Put your heads right under. You'll feel better."

A few minutes later, when twenty jars full of beans sat on the table in a gleaming row, Rick and I went out to the pump, too. It was one of those old-fashioned pumps with the long handle—just like the one at the end of the sink inside the cabin, only bigger. We took turns pumping and letting the icy cold water run over our hair and down our necks. Then we went to sit with Mom and Marcia on the porch. Mom was on the floor, leaning against the vine-covered railing; Marcia was sort of crumpled on the top step. We all looked as if we'd been fighting a jungle war—in monsoon season.

Miss Berry came out, wiping her face and neck with a wet towel, and sat in her porch chair. Incredibly, she looked as fresh and spry as ever. "Not a bad half-morning's work," she said. "For city types. There might be hope for you."

Mom smiled a weak smile. I could see now that the red was sunburn, especially on her nose. Also on her arms. Marcia was burned, too. "Was it only half a morning? I feel as if I've been out there a week." She pointed to two large baskets at the foot of the steps. They were filled with cucumbers and squashes.

I thought of the jars of beans, and groaned. "Do these get canned?"

"Pickled," Miss Berry said. "Some of the zucchini I'll bake."

Mom looked at the long, dark green squashes. "Baked zucchini?"

"Zucchini bread." Miss Berry turned to Rick. "Speaking of bread, how about bringing out some lunch. Bread's in the bread drawer, cheese in the refrigerator. You can help him, Jennifer. Marcia had better rest awhile. She looks done in."

"I can help," Marcia said. "I'm not even tired." She stood up slowly, as if all her joints had locked together. Inside, she groaned as she poured lemonade into five blue glasses. "Every cell in my body hurts," she said.

I pointed to the beans. "Look at what we did. All those." Suddenly I was very proud. Those beans would last Miss Berry all winter.

Marcia did not seem properly impressed. I gathered a cutting board, a chunk of cheese, and a knife and took them outside. No matter what Marcia had done, it couldn't have been any harder, I was sure. Or more important.

We ate lunch without talking. We were starved. Even Miss Berry ate a lot, considering how little she was. I guessed she worked it off, if today was typical. After the bread and cheese (and some pickles Miss Berry had made the summer before) we finished a bowl of blueberries, and Rick had the last of the raspberry cobbler. Then Rick and Marcia and I washed up and put everything away, and came back out.

"Can I learn to ride Gabriel now?" Rick asked.

Miss Berry shook her head. "Just sit awhile," she said, "and let your food settle."

Rick grumbled, but I was perfectly happy to rest. In fact, I would have liked to take a nap. But Miss Berry didn't look like a napper. Mom sighed, leaned back, and closed her eyes.

"I noticed that you've got some beetles on your beans," Marcia said. "Do you dust with Sevin powder?"

Miss Berry shook her head.

"I have a book that says it's good for killing beetles."

"Did you see the marigolds?" Miss Berry asked.

"How could I miss them? They're all over your whole garden."

"Marigolds work against bugs. And weeds."

"But you've got beetles!"

"Also plenty of beans. My rule about bugs is if they're slow enough, step on 'em. If they move too fast, leave 'em— they'll probably kill something else." Miss Berry leaned back in her chair, as if the conversation was finished.

Mom opened her eyes. "You've got beans growing in the corn," she said.

"Saves me putting up poles," Miss Berry said. "The vines grow up the cornstalks."

"There are a lot of ripe ones there. Would you like me to pick some this afternoon?" Mom asked.

"I leave those to dry," Miss Berry said. "By the time the corn's ready, I can pick corn and dried beans all at once."

"Clever," Mom said.

Minnie Berry just nodded. Lucifer, who had flopped down and put his head on Rick's lap, sighed an enormous sigh. A comfortable silence settled down around us, except for cicadas zithering in the woods and a huge bumblebee buzzing in the morning glories.

"What would you like us to do this afternoon?" Mom asked after a while.

"Are you sure you want to do any more?" Miss Berry asked.

Mom grinned. "I think we city types could manage a little more. We're supposed to be getting in shape, after all. What do you say, kids?"

"I'm going to learn to ride Gabriel!" Rick said.

I sighed. "I could help with the pickling."

"I could, too," Marcia said. "I finished hoeing all the pole beans this morning."

"Good," Miss Berry said.

"And I did the currants."

Miss Berry's eyes popped open, and she leaned forward. "You did what?"

Marcia lifted her chin. She, too, was proud of what she'd accomplished. "I did the currants. The whole patch was full of nettles."

Miss Berry's face set like stone. "You didn't pull them out?"

Marcia held up her arms, which, I noticed now, were covered with little red welts. "I sure did. Every last one."

"And what did you do with them?"

Marcia grinned her own version of Dad's enthusiastic grin. "I was going to bring them back so we could cook them. Nettles are very nutritious. But there were so many, I just piled them up by the fence."

"Nutritious." There was an ominous tone in Miss Berry's voice. "I suppose one of your books told you that?"

Marcia didn't seem to notice the tone. "Yes. I've made a study of edible wild plants this summer."

"I reckon the book didn't mention that nettles are *good* for currants."

Marcia's grin slipped a little. "*Good* for them?"

"I grow nettles and currants together on purpose. They're called companion plants."

"But nettles are weeds," Marcia said, her voice suddenly very small. "Just weeds."

Miss Berry pushed herself up from her chair. "Come

along, Richard," she said to Rick. "Let's see if you can handle Gabriel, or if he handles you."

She took a walking stick from next to the door and limped down the stairs. Rick and Lucifer followed her. At the bottom of the steps, Miss Berry turned back to Marcia. "I'll tell you what a weed is, missy. A weed is something that grows where it isn't wanted."

Meanwhile, Back at
...... the Homestead ......

This next part of the story I had to piece together from what Dad and Ben told me later. They didn't always agree about exactly what happened, so I refuse to take responsibility for absolute accuracy.

After we went off to Minnie Berry's, Dad waited awhile, hoping Ben would show up before the real work had to begin. Ben didn't come. Finally—noticing that the longer he waited, the hotter it got—Dad set off into the woods downhill from *Brunhilda* with his brand-new shovel. His enthusiasm was slightly dampened by the heat and the fact that he was alone, except for Czar Nicholas, who declined even to come outside.

His plan was to dig this humongous pit in the woods and then run the corrugated plumbing pipe from *Brunhilda*'s waste tanks to the pit. The whole thing would work like Minnie Berry's outhouse, only more comfortably and on a grander scale. The problem with the plan was digging the pit.

Remember when I said that the mountains were made of rock? The rock is covered with dirt and the dirt is covered with pine needles and other dry, dead things called "duff." In some places the rock is closer to the surface than in other places. The first place Dad decided to dig the pit, the total cover of dirt and duff turned out to be only about five inches. That means that after one shovelful, Dad hit rock. *Poing!* He tried another place. *Poing!* Another. *Poing!* You get the idea. Finally he found a place where he could actually dig—*shu-u-sh*—and after the first few shovelfuls, he hit—*thunk!*—a tree root.

So then he had to go find the hatchet and chop through the root before he could dig anymore. And as he tried to make the pit bigger, as well as deeper, he kept hitting more tree roots and kept having to chop through them. Naturally, the longer he worked, the hotter Dad got. And the longer Ben was gone, the madder Dad got. In spite of words like *independence* and *self-reliance*, homesteading, as Dad conceived it, involved teamwork. It was not a lot of fun alone. He kept imagining Ben standing in that cold mountain stream, catching one trout after another, having a great time. Sort of like being on vacation.

When Ben actually got back (with Buffy at his heels), he was out of breath, sweating, and miserable. He didn't have so much as a single trout to show for a whole morning of tramping up and down the banks of the stream, which was full of fish who wouldn't even look at his flies. But by that time, Dad could not be convinced that Ben hadn't been having fun.

Ben explained that he'd lost three flies in the branches of the trees and two in bushes across the stream. He explained that the only time he'd even come close to catching a fish, when a trout had actually come out to investigate his last remaining fly, Buffy had chosen that very moment to go splashing into the stream for a nice long drink. Then he explained that all morning there had been a kid who looked maybe a year or so younger than Ben working the same stream. This kid had a terrific fly rod and was wearing a fishing vest full of pockets that held all kinds of flies and line and stuff. This kid had only to flick a fishing line over the top of the stream to have enormous trout practically fighting with each other over which one could get himself caught. In spite of these explanations, Dad remained convinced that Ben had been having the time of his life.

So Dad made Ben dig and chop and dig for a while before taking another turn himself. Then, when they had settled into a routine, with Dad digging and Ben chopping, and had managed to excavate a pit about two feet across and nearly that deep—*poing!* They hit rock again. That's when they abandoned the project altogether.

That's also when the terrific fisherman, probably drawn to the spot by the cursing and swearing that had greeted the last *poing!* appeared on the scene and suggested they'd do better using a pick instead of a shovel. The kid, whose name was Jordy, also offered them some trout, which Ben would have turned down, but Dad accepted.

When they'd put the trout in *Brunhilda*'s refrigerator, Dad decided to drive back down to Stag to buy a pick. He offered to drop Jordy off at home to store the rest of the trout, and Jordy offered to ride into Stag with them and then come back and help them dig the pit. Ben, who'd taken an immediate dislike to Jordy the first moment he'd seen the kid catch a trout, changed his mind abruptly at the thought of another pair of hands for pit digging. Besides, it occurred to him that Jordy might teach him some fishing tricks and maybe lend him some flies.

With Jordy squeezed into the cab between Dad and Ben to provide directions, they headed, roaring and backfiring, back down the road we'd first driven up in *Brunhilda*. It was a longer route to the highway that ran through Stag, but it was a better road than the two ruts that went down from Minnie Berry's. That is not to say it was a *good* road. After less than half a mile, they bounced into a pothole, and the right front tire blew.

That's when Dad discovered that Quasimodo had no jack. And no wrench. He sent Ben back to get tools. While they waited, Jordy—who claimed to be as good at tire changing as trout fishing—pointed out that the spare Henry the horsetrader had provided was bald and not completely inflated. Dad decided it would get them as far as town, where they could replace it and get the other tire fixed.

"That'll cost ya," Jordy warned.

"It'll cost Henry!" Dad promised.

Jordy really did know about changing tires, so Dad let the kid do it, with Ben helping. Ben had never changed a tire before, and Dad said it was time he learned how. Dad watched. So much for teamwork.

Then, when they got started again, things went fairly well for a while. They stopped at Jordy's—a small house in the next valley—where Jordy's mother insisted on giving them sandwiches and fresh fruit. They went on, refreshed, and made it to Stag—very slowly and loudly, sort of limping on the one low tire, but they made it. Dad dropped Ben and Jordy off at the hardware store with his Visa card and instructions to buy a pick and three pairs of work gloves. (He and Ben had already raised blisters.) Then Dad went to the garage to see Henry about two new tires.

Dad refuses to say what happened with Henry, but Quasimodo didn't get the new tires until Ben and Jordy got back with the Visa card, so I don't think the tires cost *Henry* anything. The important thing was that they got the tires, though, so the trip back would be safe. Then they stopped at the drugstore for ice-cream cones and started back. From here on, I had to get all the rest of the story from Ben. Dad wouldn't talk about any of it.

All seemed to be well as they climbed slowly out of Stag. When the road evened out for a while, Quasimodo got up to its top speed of about thirty-five miles an hour. Then the road began descending. There was a sign warning trucks to use a lower gear for the next two miles, so Dad geared back to second. (Quasimodo has only three gears.) Pretty soon they were up to a scorching forty miles an hour, so Dad put on the brakes. Quasimodo slowed to twenty. He let them up; Quasimodo went up to thirty-five. He braked again, and the smell of burning rubber filled the cab. Quasimodo was still going thirty-five, so Dad geared down to first. Screaming protests, Quasimodo slowed to fifteen. They were still going downhill. Twenty. Twenty-five. Dad pressed harder on the brakes. Nothing happened. They hurtled around a curve where a warning sign said 15 MPH, tires squealing on the hot pavement. Around another curve they went, and plunged downward again. Ben put his hands over his eyes. Jordy, Ben says, was laughing like a crazy person.

When they went off the road on the next curve, they rode along the guardrail, leaving on it the last of the green paint from the right front fender. That slowed them down a bit. The next curve, luckily, sloped upward. When the guardrail ended, they only went on for another fifty yards before they hit the hemlock tree.

Henry might be a horse trader (Dad says the word is *crook*), but he'd done one thing right. He'd installed seat belts. So nobody was hurt. Nobody, that is, except Quasimodo. The steam that was gushing out from under its crumpled hood suggested major injury.

So, taking turns carrying the pick, they walked the four miles to Jordy's house, where Dad called Henry at the garage and said a whole lot of things that don't bear repeating. Henry promised to tow Quasimodo back to town and fix the radiator and the brakes for a reasonable fee. "You'll do it for nothing or you'll hear from the state attorney general!" Dad yelled. Jordy's father, who was out in the woods cutting timber, stopped work and drove them all back to *Brunhilda* in his Blazer.

As it turned out, that was a good thing, because when he saw where *Brunhilda* was stuck, Jordy's father showed them a little spring nearby, and explained how Dad could run a hose line from there to *Brunhilda*'s water tank. Then, fulfilling all Dad's predictions about the generosity of mountain neighbors, he stayed to help dig the pit. Dad told him all about the homesteading plans and asked if he knew of any land for sale. Jordy's father said he'd check around.

While they were digging, Marcia came back and disappeared inside *Brunhilda* without giving anybody a chance for introductions. A couple of minutes later, wild, Russian-sounding violin music could be heard over the *shu-u-shes, poings,* and *thunks* of the pick and the hatchet.

The Future
.... Field Biologist ....

Actually, Minnie Berry took the pulling up of the nettles rather well. She said that they made excellent compost, so Marcia could salvage the situation by collecting them and putting them on the compost heap. "Turn a bad thing around," she said, "and there's always something good on the other side."

"Always?" Rick asked.

"Some times you have to look harder than others."

While Rick had his first ride on Gabriel (who threw him off twice, with much hee-hawing, just to teach him a lesson, Miss Berry said) Marcia carried all the nettles from the fence at the far end of the vegetable garden to the compost heap behind the cabin. I'd been sent to get dill from the herb garden that was also behind the cabin, so I saw how many trips Marcia made. She could have asked Miss Berry for the wheelbarrow and done it lots faster and more easily, but she didn't. She just trudged down and back, down and back, carrying armfuls of limp nettles, a look of grim determination on her face. When she was finished, she very politely thanked Miss Berry for lunch, very politely refused a glass of lemonade, very politely said good-bye, and headed back to *Brunhilda* and her violin.

I spent longer than I needed in the herb garden. The sun was still beating down on the world, and there wasn't any shade there, but even so, it didn't seem as hot as it had been inside when we were canning. And it smelled wonderful. I mean, really wonderful. Like those little bags they make to put in drawers. It was pretty, too. The herbs were planted in patterns in a big circle.

At the outermost edge of the design there was a patch of catnip. Some of it was flattened, where Caliban, I supposed, had rolled around in it. Catnip is supposed to work on cats sort of like a drug. I nibbled the edge of a leaf. Yuck. Whatever catnip has, it isn't for people.

As I started to pick the dill, I heard a strange sound. It was a high-pitched, eerie sort of wailing. Almost as soon as it started, it stopped, so that I thought I'd imagined it. I stayed where I was for a moment, listening, to see if it would come again. Nothing but the cicadas. And Rick, around the front of the cabin, calling to Mom to watch him ride one-handed.

I reached for another sprig of dill. The sound came again. Louder, and closer. I couldn't see anything. I had just decided that it was a shame to miss seeing Rick ride a mule one-handed, and that I should hurry around the cabin before he quit doing it, when there was a movement among the day lilies that were growing next to the cabin. The sound grew louder, and Chatter emerged from the lilies, her eyes round and blue and crazy, her back arched, her tail fluffed to three times its normal size. She came toward me, stiff legged and wailing.

Now Chatter's not a big cat. Even so, I got to my feet and started backing away. She came forward a few more steps, and then sort of rose into the air—leaped upward with all four feet at once—and came down, howling, right in the middle of the catnip patch. She flipped onto her back and rolled back and forth with her feet in the air, all claws out and gleaming in the sunlight.

Behind me, I heard another sound—a deep, wavering sort of growl. It got steadily louder. I looked over my shoulder. Caliban, crouched low to the ground, his tail flipping back and forth, was creeping forward between the herbs. Chatter apparently didn't hear him. She kept rolling, her wail gradually escalating.

Before I could think what to do, with a wiggle of his rear end, Caliban pounced. As if she'd been shot from a cannon, Chatter was on her feet and running. A beige streak disappeared into the woods. A black streak followed, and I was left standing alone, sun and silence all around. I stood for a moment, waiting for the sound of the fight. Nothing. Chatter was much younger than Caliban. Maybe she could outrun him.

Then it came. Screeching and yelling and hissing. It lasted only a few moments. Silence. Then the growling started again, though not as loud as before. There was a rustle in the bushes and Caliban appeared, backing up. He growled and backed, backed and growled. Finally, when he'd gotten nearly to the middle of the herb garden, he turned around. His torn ear was bleeding. He glanced toward me, his green eyes slitted, and then stalked away, tail high. If you didn't know Chatter, you'd have thought Caliban had won.

Rick rode Gabriel around the cabin to find out what had happened. "Caliban chased something away," I told him. I let it go at that. I didn't think he'd be happy to find out that Chatter had added Caliban to her list of victims. We pickled a few jars of cucumbers next, a job that's every bit as hot and miserable as canning beans, and Minnie Berry told us to go home. I was overjoyed. There might be time to take Quasimodo and find someplace for a cool, refreshing swim before dinner. We took the cucumbers and squash Miss Berry offered us, and promised to come back the next morning—earlier, this time. Rick ran to hug Gabriel once more. And didn't come back.

"It's okay," Mom said. "He knows the way. I think he's in love."

Marcia was still playing the violin when we got back; Dad and Ben were still digging, along with a tall, craggy-looking man and a wiry, short-haired kid wearing a T-shirt and jeans that looked about a size and a half too big. The kid was chopping away at tree roots with a hatchet. Dad stopped to introduce us.

Mom shook hands with the man, Mr. Gagnon, then with the kid, whose name was Jordy Gagnon. "You look like a very capable young lady," Mom said.

Ben's jaw dropped about six inches, and his face went bright red. All this time, he'd thought Jordy was a boy.

"She takes after her big brothers," Mr. Gagnon said.

Jordy just grinned.

"I hate to leave before the job's finished," Mr. Gagnon said then, "but we'd better be getting back home. I've got some timber to haul in before dark. It's been a pleasure meeting you." He offered his hand to Dad, who shook it gratefully. "How soon will Henry have your truck fixed?"

"He said next Thursday. I guess we can manage without it for that long. Pioneer spirit and all that."

Mr. Gagnon smiled. "Thursday, eh? Good luck." He turned to his daughter. "Let's go, Jordy. Did you say goodbye to Ben?"

Jordy glanced around. Ben had disappeared. "Don't see him."

"Well, you'll see him another time." Mr. Gagnon waved his hand toward *Brunhilda,* where Marcia was now playing something complicated but mournful. "And tell your daughter she plays a mean fiddle."

They climbed into their Blazer and bounced off down the road. "Nice folks," Dad observed. "Nice neighbors. Real people."

"Pioneers," I added. "What happened to Quasimodo? I wanted to go to the beach."

"Never mind what happened, we'll have it back next Thursday," Dad said. "You can go to the beach next Thursday."

I opened my mouth, but Dad spoke before I had a chance to get a single word out. "Or you can *walk* to the beach now. Take your choice."

"Thursday," I said. "I like Thursday. Thursday's great."

Putting thoughts of Quasimodo out of his mind, Dad grinned and rubbed his hands together. "You must see what we've done. The first homesteading project! Come out here, Marcia," he called.

For the next ten minutes or so, Marcia and Mom and I had to stand at the edge of the latrine pit as Dad explained how important it would be to our future here and what an enormous job it had been.

It is not easy to admire a latrine pit, especially if you didn't dig it yourself. Big deal, is what I thought about it. "Great!" is what I said. Then, while Dad went on about duff and rocks and tree roots, I sort of edged away and leaned against a tree on the other side of a huge boulder, wishing I were on a beautiful, scenic beach on a beautiful, scenic lake.

Suddenly my day took a turn for the better. In fact, I realized it was altogether possible that my whole summer had taken a turn for the better. What happened was that Rick came bounding through the woods and behind him came—you may not believe this because for a moment I didn't believe it—that gorgeous guy I'd seen driving the Jeep down in Stag.

I will describe him all over again, in case you've forgotten him. Sandy hair, very bright blue eyes, a deep tan, gigantic shoulders and biceps. He was taller than Dad, so I guessed he was over six feet tall, and he was dressed in khaki shirt and trousers and hiking boots. And when he saw me—get this—he smiled. At me. His teeth were absolutely white and even. He could have been a movie star, he was so perfect.

"Well, well, well, if it isn't the reptile lover!" he said.

Reptile lover? I smiled back as if I knew what he was talking about. As if he were not as crazy as he was gorgeous.

"This is my sister, Jenny," Rick said.

"It *was* you I saw on the corner down in Stag, immersed in a reptile book, wasn't it?"

My mind doesn't always work very fast, but it was going like lightning right then. I thought of several things all at once. First, he'd noticed me. He'd looked at me close enough to see what book I was hiding behind and remembered it. Second, he'd remembered *me*, even though I was hiding behind that book. Third, he recognized me now, in different clothes and without the book.

I stood up a little straighter, wishing I had on my sundress instead of the shorts and T-shirt I'd canned beans in. I smiled some more, and discovered I was having difficulty breathing. "That was me," I managed to say, my voice sort of squeaking. Still smiling, I cleared my throat as subtly as I could. "This is Stan," Rick said. "He studies snakes." I smiled even more. "That's wonderful," I said. Stan's eyes sort of crinkled at the edges. And he had a cowlick above his right eye that made his hair stand up on that side and sort of fall over his forehead to the left. There were freckles on his nose and sprinkled across his cheeks. Wonderful freckles. I cleared my throat *before* I talked this time. "I love snakes. Just love them."

Before Rick could say anything, I stepped on his toe. "Ouch!" he said, and then Mom and Dad and Marcia were there, so Rick had to introduce them.

I haven't the slightest idea what anybody said after the introductions. I did notice the curly golden hair on Stan's arms, though, and the way he hooked his thumbs into his belt loops after he'd shaken hands with Mom and Dad. His shirt sort of stretched across his back and shoulders, and his rolled-up sleeves emphasized the curve of muscle in his upper arms. His boots were L. L. Bean boots, very well worn. He could probably walk twenty miles in them without getting blisters. Probably walked twenty miles in them all the time.

"Sort of a summer internship," he was saying now. His voice was deep and warm. Tingles went down my back when he talked. "It's my major. I hope to be a field biologist."

My mind was still racing. His major. He was in college. And he was going to be a field biologist. What a wonderful thing to be. Field biologists get on *National Geographic* specials. He'd be great on television, I thought, telling people about—what? Reptiles. Snakes.

"They're very rare, you know. And this is one of the few places we can find enough to study. We hope to find ways to save them."

I smiled. He wanted to save endangered species. How noble. How generous. And his eyes were so blue.

"But aren't they dangerous?"

This was Mom. How could she think a guy like Stan would be afraid of a little danger?

"Not really. They're very shy—"

"Just like I told you," Rick said.

"Your son knows a lot about animals," Stan said. What a wonderful voice. I wished he would go on talking for hours. It didn't matter what he said. "In any case, a bite is seldom fatal. I've been bitten once myself."

Bitten. He'd been bitten. How brave he was.

He turned and looked at me. "How would you like to see the den I've been watching?"

Ignoring the astonishment of my family, I nodded. Since I wasn't breathing, I couldn't actually make any sound. Den, he'd said. Snake den? Did he mean a snake den? My cheeks felt as if they were cracking with the smile I'd been maintaining all this time.

"Can I go, too?" Rick asked. "I want to see a timber rattler!"

Timber rattler. The snakes Stan was talking about were timber rattlers!

Stan mussed Rick's hair. His hands were enormous. "You wouldn't see one at the den," he said. "They leave in the spring and don't come back till October or so."

"No snakes?" My voice squeaked again.

"No. I'm awfully sorry. But I think you'll find the den interesting anyway. Rare as they are, you aren't likely to run into a rattler by accident. Of course you knew that already."

"Of course." I took a deep breath at last. There wouldn't be any snakes at the den!

"Can't I go?" Rick said. "Please?"

"Maybe next time," Stan said. There would be a next time! I stopped breathing again as Stan took my hand. "We won't be long," he said to Mom. "My Jeep's just down the road, and the den's not far away."

"You're sure there aren't any snakes there?" Mom asked.

"Absolutely. We've got radio transmitters implanted in the snakes from this den, so we can keep track of them. In fact, I had just located one when Rick, here, found me."

"You located one near here?" Dad asked. He was probably remembering his morning digging around in the woods.

"Not really. I'd only picked up its signal. I was, oh, half a mile away at the time, wouldn't you say, Rick?"

Rick nodded wisely. I suspected he wouldn't know half a mile from half a block.

"So, is it all right if Jenny goes with me? I'll take good care of her."

Mom and Dad looked at each other, for what felt like an hour, before Mom shrugged and nodded.

"We wouldn't want anyone who likes snakes as much as Jenny does to miss a chance to see a den." This was Dad.

He winked, and I felt my cheeks getting hot. But Stan didn't seem to notice. He just pulled me along after him and we started back through the woods.

Woods are woods to me. I don't go into them unless there's a trail I can see, preferably one with little signs and arrows nailed to tree trunks every few feet. But Stan seemed to know exactly where he was going, so I just went along with him, every nerve in my body seeming to connect directly with the palm of my hand, which was held firmly in his. In a couple of minutes we came out on the very road *Brunhilda* was stuck on. His Jeep sat there, gleaming in the sun. He helped me into the passenger side, then leaped in without even opening his door. "You've never seen a den before, have you?"

I shook my head. I didn't want to see one now, but I'd have died before admitting it.

He started the engine. "Good. You'll find it really fascinating."

"Fascinating," I repeated, as the car leaped ahead. In profile, he had a nose like a Greek statue.

I will spare you the description of the snake den. If you're a snake lover, you can find a book about timber rattlers and look it up. To me it looked like a hole among some rocks. And we had to leave the Jeep and walk and walk and walk to get to it. It was very disappointing. Stan didn't even take my hand while we walked.

In spite of his assurances, I kept thinking about timber rattlers the whole time. I mean, Stan was wearing those heavy boots that were obviously designed to protect him against snakebites. I was wearing shorts and sandals. It is not easy to pretend to be a snake lover when you're wearing shorts and sandals and walking around in the undergrowth on a mountain that is one of the few places in America with enough timber rattlers to study.

Stan was sorry he didn't have a flashlight with him so I could see the inside of the den, but I didn't mind. It wasn't a really huge hole among the rocks, so we were very close to each other while we were looking into it. I don't actually remember what he said, though he talked about it a long time. I do remember, though, the sandy-colored beard stubble on his cheek. I had never thought of stubble as interesting or romantic before. Possibly because Jason doesn't have any yet.

And then we were walking back toward the Jeep again, and I was straining my ears for the sound of a warning rattle that would send me leaping into Stan's arms. He'd been right, of course. There were no snakes. I was almost disappointed when we got back to the Jeep safely.

"You want to drive?" he asked.

I was doomed. When I admitted I wasn't even sixteen yet, it would be all over. Stan was in college. He'd think I was a baby. "Well—I've never driven a Jeep before."

"You drive a stick?"

"I never have."

"No sweat. I'll teach you."

That's how, with damp palms and shaking knees, I had my first driving lesson on a straight stretch of mountain road. The Jeep bucked and jolted and shuddered and stalled out, but Stan kept his cool. He told me what to do, and when I didn't do it, he just told me again, his voice sending shivers up my neck that made it harder than ever to remember what he'd said. Once, when we'd stalled out for about the hundredth time, he put his hand on my leg and told me to take it easy. I could barely think to start the engine again. But when I got it going, I managed to move ahead without jolting, and even changed gears without grinding them. Who needed a red BMW?

It was clear that with Stan to teach me, I'd be a brilliant driver. It was also clear that he was the most gorgeous future field biologist the world had ever known. And I would stay with him in the mountain wilderness forever.

.... Love and Whatever ....

Blinded by passion—or what Marcia insisted on calling my "crush" on Stan (just because he was a couple of years older than me)—I wasn't my usual sharp, observant self over the next few days. No more dreams about red BMW's, of course. Now there were dreams about Jeeps. And secluded mountain homesteads. And Stan. Beautiful Stan.

Once I had a nightmare in which Stan's face turned first into a snake and then, dropping one scale at a time, into Jason. I woke up in a sweat and lay there, unable to go back to sleep, rigid with guilt. What if Jason, off by himself all summer, hadn't met any other girls? What if he was being faithful?

By morning I had recovered. Guilt was gone, replaced by visions of sandy beard stubble and bulging biceps. It wasn't my fault. I was almost sixteen. It was hormones.

Without Quasimodo, various minor tasks once again took on the monumental proportions of pioneering projects. The prospect of a hike down to Stag for every little civilized thing anybody needed was so daunting that we quickly discovered how few things were real necessities.

First we ran out of milk and soda and discovered that it was marginally possible to drink water. Then we ran out of breakfast cereal, which we'd been eating dry, and bread. Miss Berry offered us a couple of her wonderful home-baked loaves, but Mom insisted on baking some herself—in Miss Berry's wood stove, of course. Homesteaders have to know how to do that. After two abortive attempts, she finally produced a loaf that was not burned on the outside and sticky in the middle.

Ben, who didn't come back till very late on the day he'd found out that Jordy was a girl, vanished again very early the next morning. He was gone a long time and returned with a whole bunch of trout. Between those and the ones Jordy had given us, we had a feast.

Then Ben went out again the next morning. And the next. We got very, very tired of trout, which Rick had never liked in the first place. I noticed some fungus on a tree stump one day, which reminded me of mushrooms. Smothered in sautéed mushrooms, I thought, even trout might not be too bad. But Mom vetoed my idea for a mushroom hunt. The trout remained unadorned. I developed a craving for beef and an almost pathological loathing of bones.

In an effort to provide a little variety, Mom let Rick ride Gabriel to a farm in the next valley where Miss Berry got her eggs and milk. It wasn't his fault that by the time he got back, the milk was all thick and lumpy. The heat wave was worse than ever. We decided we could live without calcium till we had wheels again. At least we had the eggs. Adirondack spring water began to taste almost good. The same could not be said for cucumbers, beans, and squash, the only food—besides trout—we had in abundance.

Mom and Marcia went back to the blueberry patch once, armed with Buffy and a couple of large sticks. Bruno didn't appear, but they were so busy watching for him, they could hardly pick berries. Marcia said it wasn't an efficient use of time.

In spite of all his talk about getting in shape by doing a lot of walking, Dad did not offer to hike down to the grocery himself. He claimed that he was too busy. In order to back up that claim, he had to find things to be busy doing, most of which had to do with minor repairs to Miss Berry's various outbuildings.

That is, they would have been minor repairs for someone who knew what he was doing. Under Dad's hand they were transformed into massive undertakings, some of which had to be done two or three times before they could genuinely be considered repairs. Patching a tiny leak in Gabriel's barn roof, for instance, took two full days.

It occurred to me that I probably didn't need to worry about living in a log cabin. If Dad tried to build it, we'd all be grown and gone before it was finished. Dad, however, seemed inordinately proud of his work. And Miss Berry did her best to hold up under his help.

Rick, who had once been a complete flake, became a paragon of hard work and responsibility where Gabriel was concerned. He fed him, cleaned his stall, combed and brushed him, and even braided his mane and tail, which looked sort of silly on a mule. He would gladly have ridden Gabriel to Stag every single day, if Mom hadn't refused his offers. She insisted that as a beginning rider, he shouldn't ride an unpredictable animal on real roads where there were real cars.

Actually, they probably would have been fine. That mule seemed to be as crazy about Rick as Rick was about him. They wandered all over the mountainsides, looking more like an eccentric centaur than a kid on a mule. Rick could have ridden Gabriel safely to Philadelphia.

Meantime, Rick's cemetery hadn't grown the way I'd

predicted. Chatter seemed to have given up hunting. She took to visiting Miss Berry's herb garden daily. While she was there, rolling and wailing in Caliban's personal catnip supply, Caliban would stay under the front porch, pretending to be asleep. Every afternoon Chatter would come back to *Brunhilda,* wild-eyed and caterwauling, to sleep it off.

From time to time Rick did some other minor chores for Miss Berry, for which she paid him with cookies and pie and fruit cobbler. None of the rest of us ever got these extra treats, because no one else was ever around when the offer was made. Marcia said Miss Berry must have been one of those teachers who always had a pet. Marcia hates teachers like that—unless, of course, she's the pet.

Which brings me to Marcia. In those days Marcia seemed to have as big an obsession with Miss Berry as I did with Stan. Only hers was the opposite of a crush. Minnie Berry was gradually driving her crazy.

At the end of a day Marcia would ask what the plan was for the next day, and Minnie Berry would say something like, "Reckon we'll handle tomorrow, tomorrow."

Marcia's idea of the perfect life is one that is planned a year or so in advance. Failing that, she wants to know exactly what's going to happen for the next month. In the Skinner family, of course, this is seldom possible, so Marcia can, on occasion, come down to planning as small a period as a single day. Less than that, and her sanity is at risk.

Miss Berry utterly refused to plan at all. When we would arrive at her place in the morning, she would look at the sky to see how late we were (I'd begun to think she never slept at all, since she was always up and doing when we left at night and always equally up and doing when we got there in the morning). Then she'd say she reckoned we could hoe for a while, or pick beans for a while, or "pickle some."

"Then what?" Marcia would ask, and Miss Berry would screw up her face and rub her chin and say, "Depends." What it depended upon was which vegetable was ready to pick, which garden patches had grown so many weeds that she'd decided it was time to hoe, how hot it was, how sunny it was, which direction the breeze was blowing, or some other variable Marcia couldn't figure out.

Marcia was convinced that such total lack of planning and organization was drastically interfering with the efficiency of Miss Berry's life, and she refused to be swayed in this conviction by the obvious fact that Miss Berry got along better all alone than most corporations with hundreds of employees. In spite of her arthritis, Minnie Berry could bake three loaves of bread and two desserts, pickle fifteen quarts of cucumbers and five of green tomatoes, keep the inside of the cabin spotless, show each of us how to do whatever chore we were supposed to do and watch over us till we had it right, make five or six patches for a quilt she was working on, and arrange fresh flowers for her table on any given day.

Marcia had admitted that Minnie Berry knew some things about homesteading. But then she decided that because Miss Berry hadn't gone to college, she couldn't know very much *except* homesteading. Marcia set out to prove this theory. Watching while Miss Berry showed her how to turn the compost heap with a pitchfork, she would say, casually, "I've been trying to remember the exact wording of Hamlet's soliloquy. I get as far as 'Whether 'tis nobler in the mind. . . .' But I forget what comes next."

" 'To suffer the slings and arrows of outrageous fortune,

Or to take arms against a sea of troubles, And by opposing end them,' " Miss Berry would say, handing her the pitchfork. "Don't forget to sprinkle that can of water on it when you've got it all turned."

No matter what Marcia quoted from her stock of classics, Miss Berry knew it. So Marcia switched to history. Miss Berry never missed a name or a date, from the Tigris and Euphrates, up through Greece and Rome, to Europe in the Middle Ages, which is as far as Marcia had gotten in school. If Miss Berry knew what Marcia was trying to do, she never gave any hint of it. She just answered and went on about her business, leaving Marcia fuming and muttering and planning a new tactic.

Finally, there was the garden. Marcia would get up early in the morning and do her research so that no matter what Miss Berry wanted her to do that day, she'd know how to do it—right. Scientifically.

But it was like the nettles over and over and over again. When she'd finished picking cucumbers one morning, she thinned an entire row of onions so there would be room for them to grow really big. Miss Berry looked at the few onions that were still there, shook her head, and explained that it had been her green onion row. For salads. The big onions, spaced properly, were somewhere else. Almost exactly the same thing happened with turnips. Marcia thinned the row that Miss Berry grew close together just for the greens.

Then she carefully raked all the pine needles off the "ever-producing" strawberries, only to learn that Miss Berry used pine needles for mulch there because it made the berries taste better. After spending a very hot afternoon gathering pine needles and remulching the strawberries, Marcia quit taking the initiative about anything and did only what Miss Berry told her to do. But you could see the strain of it behind her eyes.

Mom and I had already been doing only what Miss Berry told us. For me it was because when I didn't have to think, I could daydream about Stan. Mom did it because that way she could learn so much—how to pickle, for instance. With the amazing abundance of cucumbers Miss Berry's vines produced, we were able to make four different kinds of dill pickles, two kinds of sweet, and about eighty trillion bread-and-butter pickles, which I hated doing because we had to cut them into slices first. If my mind wandered to blue eyes and gorgeous freckles, I had a tendency to slice my fingers.

Mom was learning other things besides how to make pickles. Mainly, she was learning that whatever took a couple of minutes to accomplish in the city could take a whole day when you were homesteading. Just the pickles, for instance. They were taking us hours and hours of sweat and misery. At home, a mere three minutes in the pickle aisle at the Acme could give us as many jars, and varieties, of pickles as we could fit into a grocery cart. And a stroll through the produce section could get us onions and lettuce and beans and broccoli and anything else Miss Berry could grow, plus bananas and pineapples and coconuts and kiwi fruit besides. All without getting sunburned, breaking our backs over a hoe, or acquiring one single blister.

At home Mom manages her full-time job *and* her share of the cooking and housework. (Usually more than her share, in spite of the famous Skinner contract.) Even so, she has time to watch TV or read at night. In the mountains, Mom had trouble finding time to write her newspaper column. And when there was time, like after our nightly dinner of trout and beans and cucumbers, she was too tired from the hoeing and the weeding and the canning and the pickling to do it. She'd sit at the typewriter, and pretty soon, with her hands still on the keys, her eyes would close and her head would nod, and she'd be asleep. She'd wake up with a jerk a few minutes later and say she was going to bed.

"After all, I can't mail the column till *someone* goes down to Stag," she'd say, glowering at Dad as she headed for the bathroom to brush her teeth.

Finally, though, it was Thursday, and Dad had no choice. He had to go to Stag to get Quasimodo. While the rest of us (except Ben, who was resolutely depleting every trout stream in the Adirondack Mountains) were getting ready for our daily trip to the salt mines of Miss Berry's little homestead, Dad donned his hiking boots. He whistled cheerfully while lacing up, and set off with a jaunty wave. Buffy, who'd apparently forgotten what a hike in the mountains was like, frolicked wildly around him.

"Aren't you taking your backpack?" Mom called to him from *Brunhilda's* doorway.

"No need," he called back. "I'll be driving back." With those words, he and Buffy set off down the road.

"Thank heavens," Mom said. "Every stitch of clothing we own is dirty, and we need to go down to the Laundromat first thing tomorrow."

Chatter seemed more than usually present that morning. She was making strange, guttural sounds in the back of her throat, and we thought she'd taken up hunting again. We looked for the corpse. Not so much as a pancreas to be seen. Chatter rolled on the floor and started scooting in and out between the captain's chairs on her back. "She must have hit the catnip during the night," Marcia said. "Is there such a thing as Nip Anonymous?"

Czar Nicholas, too, was up and around. Usually, the extent of his exercise in any given day was the walk from my bed to the litter box in the bathroom, followed by the trek to his food dish in the galley. After that he'd have to spend the rest of the day curled up on the couch, recuperating. This morning, though, he was practically animated. He followed Chatter around the chairs, batting at her tail with one paw.

"Maybe it's the mountain air," Mom suggested as we got ready to leave. "It's finally gotten through to his brain."

It was very late in the afternoon before we saw Dad again. Mom and Minnie Berry had just finished making a batch of jelly, Rick was riding Gabriel in figure eights around the barn and the toolshed, and Marcia and I were sitting on the sagging porch with large glasses of lemonade, recovering from hoeing the cornfield. Dad appeared, walking very slowly, with two well-stuffed and thoroughly tattered paper bags in his arms. Buffy limped along behind him, her ears down, her tail between her legs, and only perked up when Lucifer came out to greet her.

Mom, wiping her face with her apron, came to the door. "Well?"

"Consumer fraud!" Dad said. "I'm calling Ralph Nader!"

Marcia took him her lemonade, and he dropped his bags onto the steps, slugging lemonade as he sank down next to them. Minnie Berry appeared beside Mom. "Truck not ready, eh?"

Dad just shook his head.

"I'm not surprised," she said. "Did he bother with an excuse?"

"He says his peacock caught its tail in a fan," Dad said bitterly.

"Always was creative, Henry. Runs in the family."

"First I will call Ralph Nader," Dad snarled. "Then the president."

Mom eyed the grocery bags. "What did you bring?"

"Dog and Cat Chow, hamburger, chicken—which has probably gone bad in the heat—and hot dogs."

"Hot dogs, yea, hurray!" This was Rick, who had ridden up on Gabriel. Gabriel took a meditative bite of one of the bags, and Dad snatched it away.

"I don't suppose you brought a washer and dryer," Mom said wistfully.

"I couldn't. My peacock caught his tail in a fan."

.... Wash Day ....

Stan came by the next morning and had a cup of coffee with us before he set off with his radio equipment. I don't like coffee myself, so I just drank my Adirondack spring water and watched his Adam's apple bob as he swallowed his coffee, hoping he would invite me along to chase snakes. That has to be a sign of how messed up my hormones were—I mean, chasing snakes? Poisonous snakes? But he didn't invite me. He didn't even invite Rick, who pointed out several times that this was "next time" and he ought to be allowed to go along.

"Next time I go to the den," Stan said, "not next time I track snakes. Doc Whitehead would have a fit if I took somebody with me to do that."

"He's right," Dad said. "You don't take amateurs tracking rattlers. Anyway, I'll probably need you today. I'll need all the helpers I can get."

"Helpers? For what?" Mom had gathered all the laundry, which was stuffed into pillowcases and stacked outside the door. She was planning a hike to the Laundromat. She, too, would need all the helpers she could get.

"Until that crook Henry finishes turning his infernal junk pile into a working vehicle again, I might as well use my time for something worthwhile."

"Such as?"

"Such as fixing Miss Berry's porch."

"What's the matter with it?" Rick asked.

"It sags. Dangerously. Could collapse at any moment."

"It's probably been like that for twenty-five years," Mom said. "It can sag a few more days."

"That porch will be good practice for log-cabin building."

"I need to get the laundry down to Stag."

Dad drained the last of his coffee. "Eleanor, homesteaders do not use Laundromats. Laundromats require electricity. Plumbing. Money."

Mom nodded, but her mouth was tight, and there were creases around her eyes I'd come to recognize. I'd last seen them at the end of a hot, muggy afternoon of pickling. "Are you suggesting that I do the laundry for six people, including sheets and towels, by beating them on rocks in a mountain stream?"

Stan, who thought Mom and Dad were joking, laughed. "Ecologically unsound," he said. "You wouldn't want to put detergent into one of the streams up here. Bad for the trout."

"Ben's bad for the trout," Rick muttered. Ben had grabbed a piece of bread and gone off at dawn again.

"I'm not suggesting any such thing. Miss Berry has tubs and washboards in her shed." Dad looked from Mom, to Marcia, to me. "And you have two strong daughters. It's the way laundry was done for hundreds of years. You can do it. We Skinners can do anything we put our minds to. If I can dig latrines and fix roofs and rebuild porches, surely the three of you can do our laundry."

Mom bit her lip and then smiled at Stan. "Of course we can," she said, but she didn't so much as look at Dad.

"Well," Stan said, and stood up. I had a feeling he didn't

quite know what to make of our situation, once he realized nobody was kidding. "I've got to be going. Thanks for the coffee."

I jumped up, too. "I'll come out to the Jeep with you," I said. "I'd like to see your tracking equipment."

Stan grinned. "Sure thing." As we squeezed out between the dinette table and the stove, he winked at me. And I understood what they mean in the romance books when they say "my heart skipped a beat." He'd shown me the equipment the other day, of course, but nobody else knew that.

Outside, he took my hand. "Jenny, I'm really sorry I can't take you with me today," he said. "I know how much you'd like to see a timber rattler."

"Oh, that's okay." I was pleased with my control. I didn't even choke on the words. "You heard what I have to do today, anyway—laundry in a washtub."

"What was that about homesteaders? And electricity?"

"Just an experiment Dad's trying."

Stan took my other hand. "You've got a great family. I wish mine took to the wilderness this way. They don't understand how I feel about the woods. Or about snakes." He squeezed my hands gently. "I didn't think I'd find a girl who feels the same way I do. Not such a good-looking one, anyway. I'll come by tomorrow, if it's okay with you."

Okay? Okay? I managed a nod. He squeezed my hands again and jumped into his Jeep. My fingers were still tingling when the Jeep disappeared around the bend in the road. I could learn to love timber rattlers, I thought. Good-looking Jennifer Skinner could do anything she set her mind to.

There was something ironic about what happened with

the weather that day. The unprecedented heat wave had been with us since we'd come to the mountains. The entire northeastern United States had been baking under a merciless sun—a record-breaking Bermuda high, the weathermen called it. It had been just as hot and miserable up here as the worst summer days in Philadelphia, and all through it we'd been hoeing and weeding and canning and pickling. Roasting, broiling, and boiling ourselves alive.

Naturally, at about eight in the morning on the day we had to do the laundry, a mass of Canadian air came barreling down into New England, dropping the temperature thirty degrees in half an hour and covering the sun with heavy, high clouds. So there we were at Minnie Berry's, working in a chilly breeze that Miss Berry—wearing a flannel shirt under her overalls and a sweater over them—said was "more like it."

"More like the polar ice cap," Marcia complained, up to her elbows in sudsy water that had been hot when I'd staggered down the front steps with a pail of it fresh from the wood stove. It wasn't hot now. I thought longingly of the wood stove that was keeping the cabin all toasty warm, but Dad had jacked up the sagging end of the porch and knocked out the old supports, so he didn't want anybody to walk on it until he got the new supports in place.

"How long is that going to take?" Minnie Berry asked him, eyeing the logs Dad had gathered.

"Oh, no time at all, no time at all," he assured her. He had a pencil behind his ear and a tape measure in one hand. "I just have to measure the uprights and get them cut. Once they're in place, the porch will be perfectly stable. Then we'll do the rest. That'll be purely cosmetic."

"Think I'll just take a little walk," Minnie said. "There's

a friend I haven't seen for a while." She looked over at Mom, who was sorting laundry into mountainous stacks. "Clothespins are in the bag hanging on the line. Support poles in the shed." She scanned the gray sky. "Those clouds look too high to bring rain. If you're lucky, the breeze'll have most things dry before dinner."

"Most?" I asked.

"Denims and towels take a while," she said. "Depending on how well you wring them out."

Rick, who'd cleaned out Gabriel's stall and fed him before helping Dad drag logs, was clearly ready to quit for the day. "Can Gabriel and I come with you?" he asked.

She shook her head. "No. I'm visiting a friend of mine, not yours. Anyway, your father needs you. Where's that Benjamin?" she asked Dad. "He should be helping you. Not off fishing again, is he?"

Dad nodded. "He left early. He'll be over as soon as he gets back."

"Hmmmph," the old woman said, and unclipped Lucifer from his chain. "I'll send him quicker, if I see him. The path I take goes past the best fishing spots. You'd think he'd have had enough of trout by now. Even I have."

"I don't think it's the trout," Mom said.

Miss Berry picked up her walking stick and nodded. "I see," she said. "Explains a lot."

I looked to see if Marcia knew what they were talking about. She shrugged.

"You're welcome to lunch when you get hungry." With that, Miss Berry limped off, Lucifer beside her. Caliban came around the side of the barn, black tail crooked over his back, battered ear twitching, and followed them. I wished I could go along. I didn't care where they were going or how far it was, as long as it was away from those stacks of laundry.

As Dad and Rick started sawing a log, one on each end of a two-person bow saw, I turned to the washtub that held the rinse water. Marcia had dropped two shirts and a pair of shorts into it, after rubbing them up and down the corrugated surface of the washboard. I picked up a shirt. Rick's. Stained with blueberry. I handed it back to Marcia. "Not clean," I said.

"Mom!" Marcia yelled.

We soon learned that blueberry stains do not come out of cotton/polyester blend T-shirts. Not, at least, when scrubbed on a washboard in cold water. Not even if you put detergent right on the stain before you scrub. Nor do they come out of cotton shorts. The same can be said of raspberry stains and grass stains. The skin on human knuckles, however, is not so resistant to washboards.

"What we need here," Mom said, pushing her hair out of her eyes with one wrinkled and soapy hand, "is good old-fashioned lye soap. Like the pioneers used." She said this very loudly, to be sure Dad could hear.

Dad, however, was not listening. He was cursing. Quietly, but steadily. He was holding a log in place under the edge of the porch. There was a space of about an inch and a half between the top of the log and the bottom of the porch.

"That's the second time," Marcia whispered. I noticed that her lips were blue.

"Something's wrong with this measuring tape," Dad muttered.

"I told you," Rick said, "that we were sawing on the wrong side of the mark."

Dad dropped the cut log and stood up. "Richard Skinner, I will thank you to keep your opinions to yourself. The problem, obviously, is the primitive tools we have been using. What we need is a decent power saw."

"Power saws use electricity," Mom reminded him, dropping another still-stained shirt into the basket at her feet. "Homesteaders don't need electricity. Besides, a Skinner can do whatever he sets his mind to do."

Dad dusted his hands on his jeans. "Where's Ben, anyway?" he asked no one in particular. "This is the last time he goes fishing, that's for sure. The last time!"

Ben did arrive, finally. With Jordy. Holding hands. I could hardly believe my eyes, but Mom only smiled at them. Marcia nudged me with one elbow. That's what Miss Berry and Mom had meant. Ben had a girlfriend!

Jordy, of course, was a whiz with a bow saw. She and Ben together provided almost more help than Dad could manage. He sent Rick off to ride Gabriel.

It was, again, a day full of learning. For one thing, we learned that when it's sixty degrees, breezy and cloudy, it is easier to wash clothes in hot water if you build a fire near where you're working. You can heat buckets of water and keep adding them to the washtubs, and besides, you keep warmer yourself at the same time. Rick rode back to *Brunhilda* and got a bag of marshmallows he'd hidden in his clothes bin. Even toasted marshmallows don't make this kind of laundry fun.

We learned how to wring out a sheet. It takes two people—one on each end. Being careful not to let it drag in the dirt, you twist it into a tight rope until all the water drips out. Then you hang it on the line.

That's when we learned about support poles. As soon as

we got the first sheet pinned up, the line drooped about three feet, dragging the sheet in the dirt. We had to wash and rinse and wring it all over again. This time Mom used the support pole—a long pole with a V in the top—to prop the line up. Of course she propped first, and then we couldn't reach the line to put the sheet on it, so she had to let it down again. Marcia held the bottom of the sheet while we pinned it up; then Mom pushed the pole into place. Marcia and I cheered. That just shows how skewed people's values can get in the wilderness.

Dad and Ben and Jordy kept doggedly at work on the porch, sawing and carrying logs and hammering. Ben or Jordy would say something from time to time, but Dad was in an I-am-the-father-and-I-know-everything mood and paid little or no attention to them. At last, just as I was beginning to think I was going to die, if not from the cold and wet, then from starvation, Dad announced that the porch was done.

"Supported, anyway," he said. "See? The sag is all gone."

We looked at his handiwork. Four upright logs supported the corner of the porch. Two were slightly shorter than the others, but wedges had been driven in to make up for the difference. It was not a pretty job, but that end of the porch *was* higher than it had been. Quite a bit higher.

Mom squinted at it. "It migrated."

"What?"

"The sag. It migrated. Now it's on the end with the steps."

"Don't be ridiculous, Eleanor," Dad said. "The steps provide their own support. That end can't possibly sag."

"Then you've propped it too high."

It seemed prudent to have our lunch break. We went inside. The cabin was still warm, though the fire had gone out in the wood stove. We made sandwiches out of the egg salad Minnie Berry had left for us, and Rick found a fresh pan of gingerbread in the warming oven, so we ate that, too.

After lunch, warmed and fortified, Mom and Marcia and I tackled the last of the laundry with renewed vigor, while the others set to work fixing the fixed porch.

Marcia and I took turns emptying dirty water down the hole in the outhouse, as Miss Berry had told us to do, and carrying buckets of fresh water from the outdoor pump. We learned that towels are almost as terrible to wash by hand as sheets. So are blue jeans.

Over by the porch, in and around the hammering, there was a lot of talk. "I don't think we ought to take this all out," I heard Jordy say to Dad at one point.

"She's right," Ben said.

"Don't be silly," Dad answered. "This is decorative, not weight bearing." The tone of his voice did not encourage argument. There was none. The hammering began again.

Eventually we worked our way through the last of the laundry piles and the last of the detergent. Under their burden of flapping clothes and bedding, five lines drooped between the support poles. Even my mind must have been numbed with the cold. I hadn't thought of Stan once.

"We're finished," Mom announced as she poured the last of the rinse water on the fire to put it out.

"Great timing. So are we," Dad said.

The sound of a car engine, laboring uphill, turned our attention to Miss Berry's road. Gabriel hee-hawed and kicked at the fence Rick had tied him to, as an open-topped Land-Rover came into view, driven by an elderly man. Minnie Berry, wrapped in a blanket, with a man's hat pulled down over her ears, sat on the passenger side. Lucifer was on the backseat.

"How's it going?"

"Great!" Dad replied. "All done."

The words had barely left his mouth when there was a terrific crack, followed by a kind of tearing sound, several small booms, and a drawn-out, shuddering crash. We turned. The cabin sat where it always had, undisturbed. The porch, however, complete with roof, pillars and railing, lay in a splintered mass at its feet. One log that had served as a roof support dangled forlornly over the place where the steps had been.

"*Oui*," said the man at the wheel of the Land-Rover. "All done."

... The Tattered Dream ...

What happened after that was so painful for Dad that I won't dwell on the details.

Minnie Berry was surprisingly calm, considering she had never asked to have the sag in her porch fixed in the first place. She was mainly concerned about whether Caliban had come home and gone to his favorite spot under the porch. He'd have been a furry pancake if he had. We assured her that nobody had seen him. "Can't understand it," she said. "He didn't walk with us very long. I don't know where he could be."

The driver of the Land-Rover was Jacques Gagnon, Jordy's grandfather and a friend of Minnie Berry's (a very close friend, as we were to find out), who had lived on the other side of the mountain for fifty of his seventy-odd years. He didn't waste time or words, just let Miss Berry and Lucifer out, told her he'd be right back, turned his car around, and bounced away.

He came back a little while later with Jordy's father. Between them, with Ben and Jordy helping, they cleared away the rubble that had been the porch and temporarily put the steps—which had by some miracle survived almost intact—directly up to the doorway. Then they built railings on each side out of wood salvaged from the catastrophe, so that it was possible for Minnie Berry to get into her cabin.

The worst moment for Dad came when he started helping and was told, in no uncertain terms, that he'd helped enough. There were words about city people and outsiders and game playing. So much for the good mountain neighbors. That was the only time the Gagnons actually spoke to him.

He stood around for a while and then helped Marcia and Mom and me to make a pile of the bits that were too small to salvage. Those would be used for firewood. Miss Berry, wrapped in her blanket, sat in the porch rocker that, luckily, Dad had taken down before he started to work, and watched.

In spite of his age, the elder Mr. Gagnon was an amazing worker, small and wiry and very strong. Jordy's father, too, could accomplish a lot in a short time. Watching them was like watching an entire construction crew. The whole job was done with few words. It was as if they only had to look to know what to do, and as if each knew what the other was thinking.

"We'll gather some neighbors to rebuild the porch," the younger Mr. Gagnon told Miss Berry when the steps were in place and most of the rubble had been cleared out of the way. "As soon as we can." He looked directly at Dad, though he was still talking to her. "Afraid you lost your morning glories."

"They'll come back," she said. Dad, his face red, busied himself restacking scraps.

Jacques Gagnon wiped his face and neck and hands with

a large handkerchief, then shook Miss Berry's hand. "I am sorry for this happening, but it will be fixed. We will speak soon. *Au revoir, mon amie.*" (French for "Good-bye, my friend.")

"*Au revoir,* Jacques," she answered. "And thanks."

"*Pas de quoi.*" The old man smoothed his neat white mustache with one finger and turned to Jordy, who was standing next to Ben. Extremely next to him. "Are you coming, *ma petite?*"

"I'll walk, Grandpa," she said.

"Jordy!" Her father, who had started to get into the Land-Rover, turned back to her, frowning.

"I'll walk," she said firmly.

Her father shrugged. "Come soon," he said.

"Okay."

Ben grinned and took her hand. I guess he has hormones, too.

When the men had gone, Miss Berry turned to Dad. "I had a few words with Henry. You'll find that his peacock has recovered completely and your truck will be ready tomorrow."

Dad's "thanks" could barely be heard. He stood, now, his weight on one foot, his shoulders slumped, his chin almost to his chest. After all his hollering and threatening, Miss Berry had merely had a few words with Henry and accomplished what Dad had completely failed to do.

"It was no great feat. Ever since I made him repeat the fifth grade, he's been remarkably compliant." Miss Berry smiled. "There's something to be said for having taught most of the businessmen from here to Lower Stag."

"Thanks, anyway," Dad mumbled.

"Now, if someone will give me a hand," Miss Berry said, pushing herself up out of the chair. "I'll try out this new stairway design." Rick scooted to her side. "Thank you, Richard, but I'd rather you try to find Caliban for me. It's not like him to be gone so long." She looked meaningfully at Marcia. " 'Help, I need somebody.' "

Marcia just stood there. She was as taken aback as the rest of us. It seemed a very strange thing for Minnie Berry to say.

Miss Berry shook her head. "Imagine, a girl who quotes Shakespeare at me, but doesn't recognize a Beatles song when she hears one. For shame."

Marcia, her cheeks pink, went to offer her shoulder for Miss Berry to lean on.

"Thank you," Miss Berry said. She took a few steps. " 'I get by with a little help . . .' "

" 'From my friends,' " Marcia finished, as they started up the stairs.

"Leave the laundry on the line till tomorrow," Miss Berry called over her shoulder. "It won't rain."

Ben and Jordy had disappeared. I had a distinct feeling that Ben's loner days were over. Rick said good-bye to Gabriel and went to look for Caliban. Silently, Mom and Dad gathered up the tools Dad had brought. When Marcia came down the cabin steps, eating a piece of gingerbread, we went back to *Brunhilda*.

Rick came back much later, crying. "Caliban's lost. I couldn't find him anywhere!" Mom told him not to worry, that Caliban was a tough old cat who had lived all his life in the mountains, but Rick was worried about bears.

"Bears don't bother cats," Mom assured him.

Rick consoled himself by petting Czar Nicholas, who was still uncharacteristically noticeable, rubbing up against everybody's legs and getting decidedly in the way.

After dinner that night, during which Dad said not a single word, he called a family meeting. It was chilly and damp in *Brunhilda,* so we all huddled together in the living room. I thought longingly of Minnie Berry's stove.

When we were settled, with Czar Nicholas in Rick's lap and Buffy at our feet, Dad cleared his throat. "It's over," he announced. "We're going home."

This was such an astonishing statement that we all just sat there, staring at him.

"It's been a mistake from the very beginning. We don't belong out here. We are civilized beings. We are returning to civilization."

And then we were all talking at once. Rick said something about Gabriel. Marcia reminded Dad about the failure of technology. Thinking of Stan, who was coming by tomorrow, I babbled something about endangered species. Even Ben, whose usual response to discord is to clam up and disappear, started in on fly-fishing.

Mom let us run on for a while. Then she spoke, very quietly. We all stopped and looked at her. "Michael Skinner, you have had a bad day." Dad started to say something, and she held up a hand. "All right, a very bad day. And I'm sorry. But you are not going to turn tail and run."

"Who said anything about running?" Dad asked. "I have changed my mind, that's all."

Mom looked around *Brunhilda*'s interior. "This is the Skinner homestead, Michael, and we are not abandoning it. I have just spent an entire day, at the expense of vast discomfort and vaster energy, doing what I could have done at a Laundromat in two hours while reading a book."

"There. You see? You don't like the pioneer life, either."

"It isn't a question of liking it. Jenny, did you like doing the laundry? Marcia, did you?"

We shook our heads.

"But we did it because of your fanatical views about homesteading. The truth is, even if civilization as we know it were utterly destroyed, washboards wouldn't save it."

"Okay. I admit it. I was wrong. The whole idea was crazy."

"You were not wrong. Fanatical, yes. Wrong, no. None of us will ever—ever—take a washer and dryer for granted again."

She was right, of course. There had been a time when putting the clothes in the washer in the basement at home had seemed like a big job to me. No more.

"More than that, we did something very few people in our world have ever done. We've accomplished important things up here, Michael, hard things. Things we're proud of. Every one of us has learned something."

"Exactly." Dad scratched at his scraggly beard. "I've learned that I like vehicles that can occasionally be counted on to get me from one place to another. I like hot water and long showers, king-size beds and a room the whole family can sit in without bruising each other's elbows."

"That is not why you want to quit, and you know it."

"I tell you, I was wrong. No one can be independent and self-reliant in the world today. We need grocery stores. Drugstores. Libraries. *Garages!* And what's so bad about that? What's so bad about calling in an expert when a job needs doing? Nobody can know how to do everything. Just because Minnie Berry has kerosene lamps doesn't mean she's independent, you know. She has to buy the kerosene. From a store! Just like regular people."

"If she couldn't buy kerosene, she'd make her own candles," Marcia said. "She knows how."

"What's the matter with all of you, anyway? I'm admitting I was wrong. I'd have thought you'd be gloating. And cheering about going home!"

"I don't want to go home," Rick said. "I want to stay here with Miss Berry and Gabriel. And, anyway, what if we went home and something happened to all the electricity?"

Dad snorted. "Nothing is going to happen to the electricity." He turned to me. "Jennifer, you *must* want to go home. Your sixteenth birthday is only a couple of weeks away. None of your friends are here. Jason—Sarah—you won't even be able to have a party."

"I could invite Sarah up for a visit," I suggested. Actually, I'd been thinking about this for several days. How would I ever get her to believe in Stan if she didn't see him for herself?

"It's your sixteenth birthday! And you don't even have access to a car."

"There's Quasimodo," I said.

"You couldn't drive that rattletrap of a moving violation even if Henry completely rebuilt it!"

"I could learn."

Dad turned to Ben. "What about you? You haven't been near your computer in two months. Aren't you having withdrawal symptoms?"

Ben shrugged. "There are more important things in life than computers."

Dad sighed. Obviously, he had not been prepared for opposition.

"Look, Michael," Mom said. "The house is rented until September. It makes no sense to go back now. And you weren't wrong about homesteading. We really were spoiled. You are suffering at this moment from a bruised self-image. And your dream of wilderness living is a little tattered. But it's too good a dream to be abandoned. Maybe it isn't right for us to move up here permanently, but we need to stay for now. This experience is valuable! Besides, if you let a little carpentry problem beat you, you'll never forgive yourself."

Dad ran a hand through his hair, and his jaw twitched. "This has nothing whatsoever to do with Minnie Berry's front porch!"

Mom just looked at him.

"I don't like it here, Eleanor. I don't like the weather, I don't like—"

He was interrupted by a sound that brought Buffy to her feet, barking, and sent Czar Nicholas, fur standing on end, catapulting from Rick's lap to the window. It was a blood-curdling scream that sent chills from my heels to the base of my skull. It sounded as if someone were being torn limb from limb. A woman. Or a baby.

"There, you see!" Dad shouted. "It's that bloody bear!"

The scream rose higher.

"That's no bear." Rick went to the door. "It's a mountain lion!"

Moments later another voice joined the first, screaming the same way, except at a lower pitch. For once, on the subject of animals, Rick was wrong. Whatever had been started the day that Chatter found the catnip and Caliban found Chatter had apparently developed into full-scale warfare. What we were hearing now sounded like the countdown to the final confrontation. As Rick opened the door, Buffy flew out past him to join the fray. Rick went after her, and the rest of us followed.

We couldn't see much. The only light was what spilled out from *Brunhilda*'s door and her living room windows. There was a scramble in the darkness, punctuated by barks and screeches. Leaves and bushes thrashed wildly. Suddenly Chatter erupted from the melee and, like a streak of beige lightning, flashed between us, through *Brunhilda*'s door, and out of sight.

Seconds later a startled Czar Nicholas, his fur puffed, plummeted down the steps and stopped at the bottom, legs spread, claws dug into the ground. He stared wildly around him. Obviously, he had not intended to be where he was. It was the first time he had set foot outside *Brunhilda* since we'd left home.

There was a yelp from the bushes, and then a howl, and Buffy backed into the light, shaking her head. In the sudden silence, Rick hurried forward and grabbed Buffy's collar.

Czar Nicholas's sudden and unceremonious introduction to the wilderness seemed to have unhinged his brain. When Mom leaned down to pick him up, he hissed at her and disappeared under *Brunhilda*. Not even Rick could persuade him to come out. Rick kept trying, though, because he was sure that Czar Nicholas could never survive a night outside. He was too old. Too lazy. Too spoiled. And Caliban was out there. If the two of them tangled, Czar Nicholas would be torn to ribbons. (He once lost a fight to a mere rat.) Finally Rick had to be forced to come inside.

Mom dabbed Buffy's scratch with peroxide, and Buffy curled up contentedly enough on the floor under the dinette table and went to sleep. Chatter, however, spent the whole rest of the night pacing from one end of *Brunhilda* to the other, muttering to herself. From time to time there would be a yowl from Caliban under the trees outside, and an answering yowl from Czar Nicholas directly beneath us.

"Makes you wonder," Marcia said as we were trying to go to sleep later, "why human beings ever took animals into their caves in the first place."

.... Party, Party ....

The next morning, dressed for his hike to town to pick up Quasimodo, Dad was quiet. Mom, on the other hand, was supercharged. "I'm glad you mentioned Jenny's birthday last night, Michael," she said as she poured herself a cup of coffee. "You gave me a terrific idea. We'll shine up your dream again and celebrate Jenny's birthday at the same time. We'll have a party."

"Party?" I asked. "How can we have a party? Who'd come?"

"Minnie Berry and Jacques Gagnon and Stan and Jordy and her family."

"Oh, no," Dad said. "I will not have the Gagnons here."

"I thought I'd ask Miss Berry to let us have it at her place."

Dad put down his cup. "I won't go."

"Don't be silly. Of course you'll go. It's your oldest daughter's birthday. Anyway, a party atmosphere will break down any barriers there are between you. City people, mountain people, we're all human. We all like good food and fresh air and birthdays. Before you know it, the whole porch thing will be forgotten."

"With everybody tripping over the rubble?"

"Jordy's father said they'd rebuild. Maybe it'll all be finished by then. You'll see, Michael—we'll make the party a celebration of all the good things about mountain living. All the things that made up the dream in the first place, the things that keep the Gagnons living up here." Dad got up and squeezed past me, leaving his coffee on the table. Mom went right on. "We'll make it a cookout. I'll do that wonderful cobbler Miss Berry taught me to make, and blueberry pie. We can have the birthday candles on the pie, Jenny! You can invite Sarah to come up for it. She can probably get a bus."

I didn't answer. A horrible thought had occurred to me. Inviting Stan to a birthday party for me would mean telling him I was only sixteen.

Marcia, on the couch in the living room, looked up from the book she was reading. "Where would Sarah stay? She couldn't come for the party and go right back home."

"Of course not. She'd have to stay awhile. Give her a chance to sample wilderness living, too."

"So where would she stay?"

"I could build her a lean-to," Ben offered.

"You could let her have your bed, Marcia," Mom said.

"And where would I go?"

"Well . . ." Mom took a sip of her coffee. "We could ask Minnie Berry if you could bunk with her for a few days. She has that little back room, you know."

"*Me* stay with Minnie Berry?"

Mom sipped her coffee. "Of course. Jenny, go write a letter to Sarah. Your father can mail it while he's in town." She pulled a folded sheet of paper from the breast pocket of her flannel shirt. "Michael, I've got a list of things you can get while you're in town. Nothing breakable."

Chatter, who had been underfoot all through breakfast,

talking steadily, if unintelligibly, sat down in front of Rick and yowled up at him.

"For heaven's sake, Rick, let her out!" Mom said.

When Rick opened the door, Chatter streaked through and disappeared into the bushes. Rick looked down. "Hurray!" he said. "He made it through the night!"

Czar Nicholas, looking entirely himself, lumbered heavily up the steps. When he reached the top, he stopped, chirred quietly, and dropped a decapitated mouse.

"Ye gods!" Dad exclaimed. "Him, too. Our animals have all become ravening killers. *This* is what wilderness does, Eleanor. Next thing we know, Rick will be asking for a machine gun."

Rick collected the remains in a napkin and took them out to his cemetery.

Dad took Ben and Buffy with him when he hiked back down to Stag that morning. The rest of us went to Minnie Berry's. High clouds still covered the sky, and it was still chilly. When we arrived, the laundry wasn't quite dry, having been wet all over again with the morning dew, but Mom said the breeze would take care of that by lunchtime.

"Caliban isn't back yet," Miss Berry said, emerging from Gabriel's barn.

"He's okay," Rick said. "He's over at our place. Fighting with my Siamese."

Miss Berry raised her eyebrows. "I'd have thought he was too old for that." She wiped her hands on her overalls. "All right, who'll do what today? Corn to hoe, carrots to can."

Later, when Miss Berry was helping us take down our laundry, Mom asked her about my party. Miss Berry thought for a moment and then grinned. "Haven't had a party here since my retirement," she said. "Jacques and the boys were planning to get the neighbors together to rebuild my porch. Why don't we combine the two and make it a real old-fashioned mountain wingding."

"We wouldn't want it to be a burden for you," Mom started.

"Darn right." Miss Berry looked from one to the other of us. "You're not the most efficient workers I've ever known, but I've got you nearly whipped into shape. I think between us, we can just about handle it. Besides, the women'll all pitch in with the cooking. That's the way these things work." She peered at Marcia, her dark eyes glittering. "Miss Planning and Organization ought to be able to come up with some plans to cover everything. Sounds like just your cup of tea. What do you say?"

Marcia didn't know whether to take this as a compliment or not, but finally she smiled. "I might be able to do that," she said.

Stuffing a folded pair of jeans into the pillowcase I was holding, I had a sudden revelation. "You know," I said, "if we made a big thing about my birthday, the people who came to do the porch—who don't even know us—might feel obligated to bring me presents or something. That wouldn't be fair. Why don't we just keep my birthday out of it?"

Mom took down a towel and turned around. "Jenny, that's very thoughtful of you. And generous." She hugged me with her free arm.

Marcia looked at me knowingly. "That's Jenny, all right. Generous to a fault."

I just smiled. Stan could come to the party now, and never know.

Around the middle of the afternoon, roaring and coughing and backfiring, Quasimodo came up the road and stopped in front of the cabin with a squeal of metal on metal. Mom, who'd been learning to make zucchini bread, came down the steps from the cabin. Buffy leaped down to visit with Lucifer, and Dad and Ben climbed out. Ben rubbed his backside. "The ride isn't much better up front than in the back."

"I don't want to hear about it," Dad said sourly. "It runs. Having now cost me the rough equivalent of a brand-new Mercedes, this truck is able to move us—slowly—from one place to another."

"Basic transportation," Mom said.

"Very." Dad frowned. "The Smiths won't budge, Eleanor."

"What?"

"That madman refused my offer to refund his rent. He says he'll take me to court if I try to get the house back before September first."

"Michael Skinner, we agreed to stay here."

"I never agreed to any such thing."

"Well, you have now. We're having the party. And it's not going to be just a little get-together for Jenny's birthday. It's going to be a porch building—a good, old-fashioned mountain wingding!"

Dad stood for a moment, looking at the pile of wood that had been Miss Berry's porch. "Count me out," he said, then climbed back into Quasimodo and roared away.

Dad went on sulking, but he had to keep it pretty much to himself once the party planning got under way. He was no match for Mom and Minnie Berry and Marcia. They made him fill in in the vegetable garden. He hoed. He picked. He mulched and composted and repaired the fence. I caught sight of him one day, when I took a batch of zucchini peels to the compost heap, standing with his hands on his hips, looking at the corn he'd just finished hoeing. For a moment I thought I recognized the look of pioneer pride, but when he saw me, it disappeared. He just wiped his forehead with his sleeve, shouldered his hoe, and headed for the cucumbers.

Stan took to coming by before he went to work in the morning and again when he was finished for the day. Late one afternoon he asked if I wanted to go with him to Stag Lake Beach. He might as well have asked if I wanted a slab of roast beef with mushroom gravy! At first I was sorry that the kids who'd made fun of me weren't there. I wanted them to see me with Stan in all his tan, muscle-rippling glory. It wasn't long, though, before I was glad the beach was deserted.

"You want to see how the water is?" Stan asked when he'd spread the blanket we'd brought from the Jeep.

"Sure," I said. I had visions of the two of us swimming together in the clear, blue water, like in those romantic movies. Lots of laughing and ducking and splashing and then lots of long, romantic embraces. I took off the flannel shirt I'd worn over my bathing suit and ran down the beach and into the water. So much for romantic visions! Stag Lake's water was the coldest water I'd ever set foot in. For that matter, the air wasn't all that warm, either. I hurried back to the blanket and put my shirt on.

"Cold?" Stan asked.

"Freezing."

So we sat on the blanket, and Stan put his arm around me. Suddenly I didn't mind that we weren't swimming. I leaned my head against his warm, strong shoulder, and we watched the sun sparkling on the water as the breeze rippled across it.

"Sitting in the sun like this is nice," I said, feeling the texture of his shirt against my cheek.

"We're absorbing its heat through our skins, just like the snakes," he said. His voice was low and soft.

"Mmmmm," I said, and realized I could feel his heart beating. I reached up and touched his deeply tanned cheek.

"You've been in the sun a lot this summer, haven't you?"

"Sure. I have to be if I want to find the rattlers. They're always looking for the sun. Without it they wouldn't have the energy to do much, you know, being cold-blooded."

Stan certainly wasn't cold-blooded. His hand was warm on my arm, even through my shirt. I looked into his eyes. They were almost the same color as the lake. "I love summer," I said.

He looked off at the blue gray ridge of mountains in the distance and smiled. "It's a very special time of year, you know. When it's warm up here. An important time—"

Possibly the most important time in my life, I thought. For certain the most romantic.

"Timber rattler mating season," he said.

I had an impulse to ruffle his hair, which was moving a little in the breeze, but I resisted.

"One of the reasons they're nearly extinct, though," he went on, "is that only a third of the females—"

He talked for quite a while, but I can't tell you what he said, because I was only aware of the sound of his voice and the feel of his arm around me as the sun began to disappear behind the mountains and the light changed to a soft orange and then to the silvery gray of dusk.

Then he said he thought we'd better get back. "It's getting chilly, and I wouldn't want your parents to get worried about you."

"They aren't worrying," I assured him as he helped me up.

Then, just as I'd been hoping he would, he took me in his arms. And kissed me. It happened so fast, I barely had time to kiss back. "I've got an idea," he whispered in my ear.

"What?" I asked, hardly breathing.

"You can come back with me to the lab. Doc's working tonight, and I can introduce you. And show you the specimen I caught this morning. We implanted his radio transmitter this afternoon."

Even through the romantic haze, I realized that the specimen he wanted to show me was a timber rattler. "Oh, Stan," I said, thinking as fast as I could with his arms still around me. "I'd love to. I'd really love to. But I just remembered that Mom told me to get back before dark. She— wants me to—to do something for the party we're having," I finished lamely.

"Okay," he said. "Another time."

I nodded, and he kissed me again. This time, I was ready. His cheek was rough against mine. A wonderful sensation!

Over the next couple of days, I got very good at thinking up excuses for not meeting Doc Whitehead or any of Stan's beloved specimens.

Marcia, meanwhile, was in her element. All her planning instincts were working overtime. Jacques Gagnon took her

and Miss Berry around to talk to all the people who were
coming to the party, and she made endless lists of foods
people were going to bring and activities for the kids. She
borrowed a huge, hand-cranked ice-cream maker and some
folding tables and chairs from the church Jordy's family
belonged to. She got someone to contribute a pig for roasting and someone else to lend a wagon that Gabriel could
pull for hayrides. She was so caught up in the party that
she was glad she'd be staying at the cabin to keep an eye
on things. She didn't trust Minnie Berry to remember
everything.

After Sarah had had time to get my letter, Stan took me
down to Stag to call her. She already had her mother's
permission to come and had checked out the bus schedule.
She would arrive in Lower Stag (ten miles south of Stag)
at noon on the day before my birthday. She could stay five
days.

I was very proud of myself. During the whole call, I didn't
even mention Stan, who was waiting in front of the phone
booth, leaning on his Jeep. I wanted to surprise her.

As it turned out, the Adirondacks did, too.

Sarah Confronts
...... the Wilderness ......

When Dad and I arrived at the bus stop in front of the drugstore in Lower Stag at twelve-thirty on the coldest, grayest August day in recorded history, Sarah was sitting on her suitcase, shivering in a sundress, stockings, and heels. As Quasimodo slowed to a stop, backfiring and squealing, she looked about ready to pick up and run.

"It's us!" I shouted, leaning out the window so she could see me. "Sorry we're late." We'd misjudged the distance and Quasimodo's willingness to take us that far.

While we were hugging, Sarah looked over my shoulder at Quasimodo, as if she were seeing a living *Tyrannosaurus rex*. "This is it? This is your truck?"

"Basic transportation," I said.

"R-R-Right." Her teeth were chattering.

I was dressed in jeans and a sweatshirt, with my denim jacket over that, and I'd been cold the whole trip because the window on the passenger side was stuck halfway down. "Why don't you have a sweater on?" I asked her.

"I don't have one that matches," she said, as if I'd taken leave of my senses.

"Sarah, you are in the mountains. Color coordination is not a survival issue. Why'd you wear a sundress, anyway?"

"It was hot in Philadelphia." She scanned the heavy, dark clouds. "And sunny. You know—like August. What month is it up here, anyway—November?"

I looked at her eye shadow, her matching lipstick and nail polish, and the small white purse that hung over her shoulder on its tiny white strap, and shook my head. "You're going to have to give a little," I told her.

Dad had already thrown her suitcase into the back of the truck, but I made him get it out again. Then, when I had assured her that no one in the village of Lower Stag would ever see her again, or be important to her future life in any way, she consented to put on her one and only sweatshirt. It was pale yellow, with the head of a lion outlined on it in gold glitter. "It clashes with my dress," she complained.

"No one will notice," I said. "And even if they did, I promise you, they wouldn't care."

She hesitated about climbing into the truck, but when I told her that the only alternative was to walk sixteen miles, or else to ride in back with her suitcase, she squeezed in next to Dad, and I got in after her.

So began the longest trip of my life. Or Sarah's. Or Dad's. We weren't out of Lower Stag when it started to rain. In moments the rain had become a downpour. Luckily, the windshield wiper that didn't work was on the passenger side. So, while it was terrifying to sit there and peer out into a blue gray blur, I had the comfort of knowing that Dad could actually see most of the narrow, winding mountain road we were traveling. Dad's window, along with his door, was stuck permanently shut, so he was also spared the deluge of water that came in through my window and drenched my right side. I had no sooner congratulated

Sarah on being in the middle, where the rain didn't reach, when water started dripping through the roof over her head. I gave her my denim jacket to hide under. From Lower Stag to Stag, we were merely uncomfortable. In Stag, we had errands to do. "You don't go to town without running errands," I explained to Sarah. "Not when every trip to town has to be made in Quasimodo."

She waited while we bought some groceries, picked up the mail, stopped at the hardware and drug stores, and returned Marcia's gardening books to the library. We had no way to cover the groceries, so instead of putting them in the back, we stacked the bags inside with us, under and around our feet. Then we started out again and learned that there were worse things than discomfort.

The rain intensified until even the working windshield wiper was making almost no progress against the flood, and Quasimodo got a case of the hiccups. It would pause in its thunderous forward speed of thirty miles an hour, hiccup, shudder, and then move ahead, only to do the same thing all over again a hundred yards farther down the road. Dad tried giving it more gas. The hiccups got closer together. He tried giving it less gas. Better. Except that we slowed to twenty. He changed gears and was greeted with squeals of protest. And more hiccups.

A semi came up behind us, so close that all we could see out the blurred rear window was an enormous silver grille and two blinding headlights. The driver began honking— long, impatient blasts of his diesel horn. Dad edged as far to the right as he could, and the truck roared past, ignoring the double yellow center line and narrowly missing a pickup coming the other way.

"Hadn't we better stop and wait till the rain is over?" Sarah quavered. I could feel her shaking next to me, but I didn't know if it was fear or cold. Or both.

"I'm not sure I could get this blasted vehicle started again if I stopped now," Dad yelled over the hiccuping engine. Soon after we turned off the highway onto the mountain road that now looked more like a mountain stream, Dad's windshield wiper quit. Cursing, he slammed on the brakes and stomped on the clutch. The clutch pedal, which Henry had soldered back in place, snapped off, and the engine stalled. We sat there for a moment, saying nothing. The rain poured steadily down, and the wind howled in the treetops.

"Welcome to the clean and simple life," Dad said.

"Mmmph," Sarah said.

"You'll have to let me out," Dad explained, "so I can fix the wiper."

So we climbed down into the mud, let him pick his way out over the grocery bags, and then climbed back in. Now Sarah was as wet as I was. We dripped onto the bags at our feet. Dad fussed with the wiper for a while and then lifted the hood. "I'm going to try to adjust the carburetor while we're stopped!" he yelled. A flash of lightning turned everything blue white. Thunder crashed almost immediately as the light faded, and Dad ducked. He let the hood drop. "Never mind," he shouted. "I'll just murder Henry later." He came slipping and sliding through the mud to the door.

Sarah had my denim jacket pulled completely over her head now. "Come on, Sarah," I said, and nudged her. "We have to get out so Dad can get back in." She didn't move.

Or say anything. She just pulled the jacket tighter and sat there. "Sarah! We have to get out."

She mumbled something about lightning, just as another flash and another earth-shattering thunderclap pounded down on us.

"Let me in!" Dad shouted, and banged on the door next to me.

"Sarah!" I was past nudging now. I jammed her in the side with my elbow. "We have to get out—now!"

She pulled my jacket off her head. "I'm not going out there to get hit by lightning. It's dangerous to stand under trees in a storm."

"This is the woods!" I shrieked. "There's no place else to stand."

Dad was pounding on my window. "Okay!" I hollered at him. He'd just have to climb over Sarah. The main thing was to get him inside. I pulled on the door handle. Nothing happened. I shoved the door with my shoulder. Still nothing. Dad was pounding more furiously now. I took a deep breath, jammed my feet into the hamburger, and threw my whole weight against the door.

The door opened suddenly and I went with it, knocking Dad off his feet. In the ghastly light of another lightning bolt, I saw him fly backward, break his fall with his right arm, and then slide, head first, off the muddy road into the torrent of water roaring down the drainage ditch. Thunder drowned out whatever sounds he made on his way down. I ended up on my hands and knees in the mud.

Sarah, jolted out of her paralysis, scrambled out and helped me up. Then we slid down the bank to where Dad lay, half in and half out of the water. I reached for his hands to pull him up and he yelped. "Broken arm," he shouted.

I crawled around behind him and took hold of his shoulders. Sarah pulled on his good arm, and we got him upright. "Sprained ankle!" he shouted.

Somehow, with me pushing and Sarah pulling, we got him up to the truck, hobbling on one foot. Sarah supported him while I climbed in, and then we pulled and pushed him onto the seat. Sarah got in and shut the door. We sat, listening to the fury of the storm raging around us. "What'll we do?" I asked when things quieted down a little.

"You drive," Dad said. "I can't."

I shook my head. This was Quasimodo, not Stan's Jeep. Even Dad could barely persuade this thing to run.

"Drive," Dad repeated. "You can do it."

"Try, Jenny," Sarah said in her most encouraging voice.

So I tried. I really did. In spite of there being no clutch pedal, I got the clutch in. The engine coughed and spluttered and then started. I sat for a minute, my left foot on the clutch, my right on the brake, working up my nerve. Then, slowly, I took my foot off the brake. That's when I discovered the problem of starting on a hill. Stan hadn't told me about that. We began rolling backward. I slammed the brake on again. How could I get my right foot onto the gas pedal without taking it off the brake? I needed another foot!

"You've got to be quick!" Dad said. "Get your foot on the gas pedal fast and let the clutch up at the same time."

I tried again. As we started to roll backward, I jammed my foot onto the gas. The engine raced and we rolled even farther. I let up the clutch. Too fast. We jolted forward and stalled.

"Try the emergency brake," Dad suggested.

The emergency brake was not one of the things Henry had fixed.

I sat there with my hands curled so tightly around the steering wheel that I couldn't let go. The storm was moving on. Lightning flashed less often now, and the thunder came long afterward. I took a deep breath and tried again. This time, I got the gas on and the clutch up, but the tires just spun in the mud. I jammed on the brakes, forgetting the clutch, and we stalled again. I couldn't get the engine started again. Quasimodo coughed and choked and died.

Suddenly Sarah reached down and took off her muddy shoes. "All right!" she said, and winced as thunder rumbled above. "We'll walk. Never let it be said that I can't cope with a little hardship." She gritted her teeth, opened the door, and jumped out. "We'll carry you if we have to, Mr. Skinner."

"That a girl!" Dad said. "Way to go!"

The rain had settled now to a steady drizzle. Sarah put on my denim jacket, got a pair of sneakers out of her suitcase, and helped Dad back down. We put him between us with his good left arm over my shoulders and started walking, Dad half-limping, half-hopping. After a while Sarah and I changed places.

I've heard that winter in the Adirondacks is dangerous. Really life threatening. Well, let me tell you about August. In the rain. With wind. And a wounded man. "You okay?" I asked Dad a couple of times. His face was all creased with pain.

"I'll make it," he said.

"A genuine pioneer!" I said.

"A Skinner can do—" he said.

"Anything he sets his mind to," we said together.

Slipping and sliding in the mud, we struggled valiantly upward. Then we hit the fog.

"Fog," Sarah said observantly. Then, "Cold fog!"

"Clouds," Dad corrected her. "We're that high."

Now it felt as if we were walking through a chilly gray ocean. The air was so full of water, I could hardly breathe.

Finally we came out from under the trees and into the high meadow. Except that it was lighter, we couldn't tell the difference. We could barely see the ground at our feet to be sure we were still on the road. I thought of the cliffs. We had to be very sure we stayed in those ruts. Good old ruts. Then I thought of Bruno. Where did bears go in the rain? I hoped fervently that they went back to their caves. I was glad I hadn't told Sarah about Bruno.

Just when I decided that we'd taken a wrong turn and had become hopelessly lost, just as I became convinced that we would all die of exhaustion and hypothermia (a nice word for freezing to death), I saw a light through the fog. Then I heard Lucifer barking. And then Mom was there, and Stan, who practically lifted Dad and carried him into Minnie Berry's cabin.

After that came hot chocolate and oatmeal cookies, blankets and towels. And introductions. (I'd missed Sarah's first glimpse of Stan out there in the fog, but was perfectly satisfied with her reaction to him in the soft glow of the kerosene lamps.) Stan had been just about to come out looking for us. Now he insisted on bundling Dad into the Jeep and driving him to the emergency room at the medical center thirty miles away. Mom went along.

When it was clear that everyone was going to survive, Marcia started worrying about the party. "What if it doesn't stop raining? We don't have a rain date."

"It'll stop before midnight," Minnie Berry said. "Clear before morning."

"How do you know?" Marcia asked.

"Trust me."

Back in *Brunhilda* that evening, we learned that Dad's pioneer spirit, reawakened by our heroic trek over the mountains, had been dampened again at the medical center. His wrist turned out to be merely sprained, and his ankle badly twisted.

Still, everybody was proud of us. Especially of Sarah. We let her have all six gallons of hot water for her shower. She'd walked nearly five miles in rain and mud, totally ruined a good pair of panty hose, almost frozen to death, and met the most beautiful future field biologist in North America with her mascara running down her cheeks. She deserved a little pampering. Of course, she didn't quite realize that four minutes of lukewarm shower was pampering, but the rest of us did.

When we were finally settled in Marcia's and my beds in the tiny back bedroom, I reached across the narrow aisle and patted Sarah's arm. "Thanks for coming," I said.

Chatter, who had been uncharacteristically calm and friendly lately, leaped gently onto her bed and snuggled down in the crook of her knees. "Wouldn't have missed it for the world," Sarah said.

I patted Czar Nicholas, who was snoring quietly next to me. "I'm sorry the first day here was so terrible."

Sarah sighed and pulled the blanket up under her chin. "Oh, well, look at it this way. Things couldn't get worse."

"Don't say that," I started, then closed my mouth. It wouldn't have mattered. She was already asleep.

.... Sixteen ....

Brilliant sunshine woke me very early. As Minnie Berry had predicted, the rain was gone. My birthday. I lay in bed, listening to what passes for silence in the woods in August—crickets cricketing away, an occasional bird call, sudden bursts of wild cawing from the crows. The fact is, the natural world is never really quiet, no matter what city people think. I reached out to pet Czar Nicholas. He wasn't there. He wasn't on Sarah's bed, either. Chatter was, though, curled in a ball with her nose tucked into the curve of one black-tipped paw.

Sarah was still asleep, so I just stayed where I was, savoring the fact that it was my birthday. Sixteen. A whole new world would open up to me now. I was sixteen! Did I feel sixteen? Grown-up? Ready for a whole new world? Not really. I turned over and punched my pillow. Here I was, on the most important birthday I'd ever had, and I didn't feel any different than I had yesterday.

Then I thought about the party. A real mountain wing-ding, Minnie Berry had called it. And I looked at the golden stripes the sun was making on the wall next to my head. My best friend was here and Stan was coming. I threw off my sheet and sat up. This was going to be the best day of the summer! It was time to get it started.

Over at Miss Berry's the day had started long before,

when the sun hadn't even cleared the mountain behind her cabin. Jacques Gagnon had arrived in his Land-Rover in the semidarkness to dig the pit and get the fire started for the pig roast. He brought the pig along, butchered and dressed, but whole. Marcia, who was already up, stoking up the fire in the wood stove, told me later it was a good thing Rick wasn't there when the pig came. "It didn't look like pork, it looked like pig. Snout and ears and little curly tail."

Miss Berry had gotten up in the dark and begun making bread by the light of the kerosene lamps. Now she was kneading the dough on the round oak table. Marcia, dressed in jeans, flannel shirt, and hiking boots, came in from helping unload the pig. "Can you get along without me for an hour or so?" she asked.

"Reckon I can manage. You have a plan you haven't told me about?"

"A surprise for Jenny. I got the idea while I was outside just now." She slipped a book into her backpack. "Be back soon."

Meanwhile, back at *Brunhilda,* life was finally stirring. Between them, Mom and Stan had managed to get Quasimodo home the night before, and she and Ben were getting ready to drive down to pick up the folding tables and chairs. They planned to stop by the Gagnons' on the way to get Jordy to help.

"Be careful with that beast," Dad warned. He was sitting on the sofa bed with his foot propped up on pillows and his arm cradled in his lap. "Something's screwy with the carburetor."

"I'll have Jordy's father take a look at it," Mom said. "Because of your wrist," she added quickly.

Dad looked down at his bandaged wrist. "Right." He held it up then and smiled. It was the first smile I'd seen on his face in days. "Be sure to tell Jordy's father about the accident. And her grandfather. Be sure to tell them why I won't be able to help with the porch." He shifted his foot on the pillows. "And offer my apologies."

"Right." Mom turned to me. "Happy Birthday, Jen."

"Thanks."

Sarah was in the bathroom. She'd been there since about ten seconds after she woke up. I hadn't had time to tell her about the crucial need in *Brunhilda* to take turns. Rick finally had to hurry outside to the bushes.

"An amazingly tiny room," she said when she emerged at last, blusher, eye shadow, and every hair in place. "Barely room for a cosmetic bag. It takes ingenuity to avoid standing in the litter box."

She had just squeezed past me in the galley and said good morning to Dad, when Rick came back in, accompanied by Buffy, who had been visiting bushes with him. Buffy jumped up to greet her.

"White jeans aren't such a good idea up here," I said while Sarah changed clothes. "Especially after a rainstorm."

Sarah smiled bravely as she stepped into the only other pair of jeans she'd brought—the yellow ones that matched her now filthy, sodden sweatshirt. "Oh, well, as you said, color coordination is not a survival issue."

Fifteen minutes later Sarah was the one who opened the door when Czar Nicholas wanted to come in. He proudly dropped the second hunting trophy of his life—a limp, wet, slightly chewed mouse—directly onto her bare toes. Sarah is not fond of rodents, live or otherwise. It took fifteen min-

utes and a cup of hot tea to calm her down.
Watching Sarah sip the tea, I realized that she would not
properly appreciate Stan's occupation. I doubted that even
his gorgeous eyes and bulging biceps would make up for
the effect on her of the word *snake*. I would talk about Stan,
of course. But I resolved to avoid mentioning timber rattlers.

"Jenny," Dad said when Sarah had recovered sufficiently
to eat a little breakfast. "I have a birthday present for you."
He reached into his pocket with his good hand. "It's not
much, I'm afraid, but the best I could do under the circumstances." Something glinted in the sun. It was a brass
key ring, with a shiny new key. "To Quasimodo," he said
with a little shrug. "Sorry. Happy Birthday."

A key! My very own key! Suddenly I felt sixteen after all.
I had wheels. Even if they were on Quasimodo. I gave Dad
a hug and a kiss. "Thank you, thank you, thank you!"

Then Sarah brought out her present, *How to Write a
Marketable Book.* Sarah doesn't actually write but feels sure
that if she did, she'd produce masterpieces. She has often
pointed out flaws in *my* books. She had read this work
herself, of course, to be sure it supported her own ideas,
and would have been perfectly happy to spend the rest of
the morning discussing literary techniques. It isn't that I
didn't appreciate her present. I did. Like I said, I've used
it the whole time I've been writing this book (except when
I disagree with it, like when it says not to talk directly to
the reader). But I wanted to get over to the party.

Rick, who had buried the mouse in record time, was in
a hurry, too. He was to be in charge of giving rides on
Gabriel and was hoping he'd get to drive the hay wagon,
too.

"You coming?" I asked Dad.

He shook his head and held up his wrist. "I'll be along later. There's not much I can do, anyway."

"Is your ankle okay? Should I send Mom back to pick you up?"

Dad waggled his foot. "I think I can manage. Go along, now."

As we walked, I took deep breaths. The air was full of the scent of balsam and pine, and the sun was bright overhead. The sky was a deep, clean, jewel-toned blue. It was almost as if the mountains were apologizing to Sarah for greeting her so unpleasantly. "Isn't it gorgeous up here?"

Sarah didn't answer for a moment. She was untangling her charm bracelet from a branch. "Gorgeous," she said finally. "But muddy." She was wearing her sneakers, still wet from the night before. Already her jeans were spattered from cuff to knee.

"We're almost there." We could hear the unaccustomed sound of voices from the direction of the clearing. The whine of a power saw split the air.

"Electricity," Rick shouted. "Somebody brought electricity!"

He and Buffy ran ahead, and Lucifer came barking to meet them. Caliban, too, had come out by the time we reached the clearing. The big cat left Rick and came toward us, and Sarah stepped quickly behind me. "Don't worry," I assured her, "he won't jump on you."

I barely recognized the scene in front of us. Four-wheel-drive vehicles jammed the space between the road and the barn, and tables were set up in ragged rows from the vegetable garden to the woodpile. Kids of all shapes and sizes ran here and there, yelling and laughing. Some of them had chunks of watermelon and were spitting seeds at each other.

The generator was set up in front of the cabin, and a man was at work with a power saw. Ladders leaned against the cabin on either side of the door, and the temporary steps had been taken down. Two men were unloading lumber from a pickup truck. Jordy's father and grandfather were working together, setting the uprights for the corners.

Minnie Berry limped toward us, carrying a cake pan in one hand and a bowl of peaches in the other. She was wearing an apron over her faded overalls, and her white hair frizzed wildly around her face. "It's about time you got here," she said to Rick. "Kids are lined up to ride that infernal mule, and he's decided to be ornery. Get on over and see what you can do with him." She held the pan out to him, and he took a piece of gingerbread as he went. She turned to us.

"Good morning, Sarah. And Jennifer. Slept in after your hard day, I see."

Sarah glanced at me, her eyes wide. It was ten after nine. For Sarah this was practically the crack of dawn.

"Slugabeds, that's us," I said. I took a piece of gingerbread for each of us. "What can we do to help?"

"The birthday girl doesn't have to help," she said. Then she shoved the bowl into Sarah's hands. "You can, though. Take these to that woman down there in the red shirt. And don't let anybody steal one on the way." She started away and then turned back. "Yellow trousers? That outfit won't last ten minutes around here."

When she'd gone, Sarah looked at the peaches she was holding, then down at her clothes.

"You'll get used to her," I said.

"Right."

"Oh, look, there's Mom and Jordy. Come meet Ben's girlfriend."

"Ben's got a girlfriend?"

"Yeah. Jordy Gagnon. Over there."

Sarah squinted in the direction I was pointing. "Near that boy in the baseball hat?"

"Not near him. He's her."

The morning went quickly, and most of it was fun. Minnie Berry had been right about Sarah's clothes, though. First she accidentally got into the middle of a seed-spitting war between mountain kids and Stag kids. Then a little boy refused to listen to Rick and hit Gabriel with a stick. Sarah just happened to be between Gabriel and the barn. I was proud of her, though. Instead of running, she grabbed at the reins and stopped him, just as the furious mule was about to scrape the kid off his back in the doorway. After a futile attempt to brush the mud off her jeans, she shrugged. "When in Rome . . ." She took a piece of watermelon from a table nearby and spit seeds at the kid she'd saved.

The porch went up so fast, it was like watching time-lapse photography. By the time everybody was beginning to think about lunch, the supports were all set, the roof was in place, and they were nearly finished with the floorboards. "It's amazing what teamwork can do," I told Sarah.

"And power tools," Dad pointed out. He'd arrived, finally, limping only slightly, but with his arm in a sling made from a red farmer's handkerchief. A subtle touch.

During the morning, something else had been happening

that we found out about only later. Marcia had come back from her early-morning hike and gone into the storage shed with her backpack. After a while Miss Berry went to see what was up. She found Marcia cleaning and sorting mushrooms.

"What's this?" she asked.

"My birthday surprise for Jenny. She loves mushrooms. After all that rain, there were lots and lots in the woods. I'm going to fry them in butter and give them to her for lunch."

Miss Berry looked over Marcia's collection. "How did you know which ones to pick?"

Marcia pointed to a mushroom book, lying open on the shelf next to her. "I had my field guide."

Miss Berry picked up the book and shook her head. "You can't trust the description in a book when you're mushroom hunting. 'Good' mushrooms have killed people."

"You and Mom! You don't have to worry." You'll notice that Marcia didn't actually *tell* Minnie Berry that Mom had forbidden mushroom hunting. "I didn't pick any death caps, I promise. Besides, I didn't just trust descriptions. There are photographs, too."

"You can't trust photographs, either. With mushrooms you can't even always trust experience. I knew a county extension agent who nearly died once when he ate mushrooms his wife had picked. She had him check them over before they were cooked, just to be safe, and he said they were fine. They weren't fine!"

Marcia probably set her jaw the way she does when she's sure about something. Even though she and Minnie Berry were getting along better, this was Marcia's sore spot. Miss

Berry was questioning her books. Her trusted sources. "These mushrooms *are* fine. And I'm fixing them for Jenny!"

I suspect Miss Berry set her jaw, too. "All right, young lady. If you're so sure of yourself, how about a little test? You cook a couple of these mushrooms. Then eat exactly one bite. No more. An hour later, if you're still feeling all right, you may go ahead and cook the rest and serve them to your sister."

Marcia is stubborn. If Miss Berry had handled the situation any other way, she would probably have cooked the whole batch, and served them to me, no matter what. But this was a challenge. This way she could prove she was sure enough to eat them herself, and at the same time validate her beloved library research. "Okay. I'll cook two. Jenny can have the rest."

"We'll see."

And we did. When people had gathered at the tables, their plates weighted down with roast pork and corn on the cob, fresh bread and tomatoes, cole slaw and cucumbers in sour cream, potato salad and watermelon, Marcia came staggering out from behind the shed. Her arms were crossed over her stomach, and she was weaving as if she were drunk. "Miss Berry!" she called. "Miss Berry, help!"

A hush fell over the crowd. Even the little kids shut up. Mom and Miss Berry both jumped up and started toward her. Too late. Marcia fell to her knees and vomited. Then she started to cry. By that time Mom had reached her. Miss Berry got there a moment later. They cleaned her up with Miss Berry's apron and, between them, got her up the stairs and across the nearly finished porch, into the cabin.

They gave her a glass of water and a dose of Pepto-Bismol, and put her to bed. She went almost immediately to sleep, but Mom says that just before she drifted off, she opened her eyes. "You were right," she whispered to Miss Berry. "Again."

.... Hero ....

Once it was clear that Marcia wasn't going to die of the mushrooms, the party went on. Vast amounts of food disappeared. "Mountain air must make people hungry," Sarah observed, finishing off her second helping of roast pork and her third of potato salad. "Living up here could wreck your figure."

After lunch, Ben and Jordy helped Rick hitch Gabriel to the hay wagon and the three of them supervised a ride up to the high meadows to pick blueberries. They piled lots of rocks into the wagon for ammunition in case the bear showed up.

"Bear?" Sarah asked. "Bear? You mean those very large animals with huge teeth and claws? Like in the zoo? I thought they were extinct in the wild."

"No. In Philadelphia, maybe, but not in the wild."

"Here, huh?" She looked around suspiciously. "Real live bears . . ."

"One bear," I said. "Very old and very shy. And all you need to remember is 'boogah, boogah.' "

"This shy old bear isn't in the habit of attending parties, is he?" she asked.

"I don't think so."

"Good, then. I'll just stay right here."

Sarah and I helped clean up when the men went back

to finish the porch. Then we took turns cranking the handle on the ice-cream maker so that there would be peach ice cream when the work was all done. While we cranked, I talked about Stan. About his eyes, his muscles, his gorgeous tan, his beautiful, deep voice. Then I told Sarah about the evening on the beach.

She listened until that last part. Then she stopped cranking. "What about Jason?" she asked.

"Jason?" I repeated innocently. "What about him?"

"Jennifer Skinner, you know perfectly well what about him."

"He's off all by himself on a college campus," I said. "How do I know what he's doing? He's probably dating some little blond with a turned-up nose. Or some green-eyed redhead. Anyway, he hasn't written for weeks."

"Maybe he doesn't know where you are."

"He knows."

She started cranking again. "All right. Go on. Then what?"

"Then he kissed me again." I mentioned the moon coming up. I mentioned the roughness of Stan's cheek against mine. I did not mention snakes.

Then I told her all about his Jeep, and the time he let me drive it. And I said he was a field biologist. I never actually told her he collected butterflies and wildflowers, not in so many words. I said he collected specimens of endangered species, and then casually referred to a couple of rare flowers and a butterfly. Can I help it if Sarah is the type who jumps to conclusions?

When we'd finished with the ice cream and the whole thing had been set in a wheelbarrow full of ice in the shade, Stan arrived. He was his usual, heart-stoppingly gorgeous self. Sarah eyed him critically as he came up from where he had left his Jeep. "Jennifer, in the sunlight he looks practically *old*," she whispered.

"Mature," I said, "and whatever you do, don't talk about age!"

Once Stan arrived, I didn't pay much attention to the party anymore. Or Sarah, for that matter. So maybe what happened really was my fault.

The thing is, Stan asked me to go for a walk with him and—naturally—I went. Sarah said she didn't mind. After we left, she hung around for a while watching some women who were helping Minnie Berry piece together her patchwork quilt. Sarah was not having fun.

Neither was Dad. Except for the food, the party had very little to offer him. All the men were working on the porch. He wandered around for a while, limping noticeably, his red sling prominently displayed. Only Jordy's mother even offered any sympathy.

He decided to go back to *Brunhilda*. However, his ankle hurt, and it seemed a long way to walk. So, when he saw Quasimodo where Mom had parked it, he climbed in and, being tired from the previous day's ordeal, went to sleep.

Meanwhile, Stan and I had been walking through the woods, talking about snakes. At least he'd been talking about snakes. We came to a stream and stopped next to a little waterfall.

"Pretty," I said.

He glanced at it. "Not as pretty as you."

My heart thudded. What a birthday this was!

He took me in his arms. "I've got a surprise for you," he said. "I have to get back to the lab, but Doc Whitehead has given me permission to take you over there with me. I caught Number Thirty-one this morning. We haven't seen her since last year. You can watch us weigh and measure her—"

"Oh, no!" I said. "I mean I can't," I added, madly trying to think of a reason. "Sarah!" That was it. "I can't leave my friend."

"She can come, too!"

I thought about this. I envisioned Sarah walking into a lab full of timber rattlers, to watch Number Thirty-one get weighed and measured. I almost laughed. It was too ridiculous.

Then I envisioned *myself* walking into that lab. Then I thought of all the conversations Stan and I had had since we'd met. All those wonderful, romantic talks. Every one of them had been about snakes.

Something snapped in my mind. This guy who was holding me in his arms was a snake nut. No matter what he looked like or how well he kissed, how manly he was or how strong, he was a snake nut. More than that, he thought I was one, too.

I looked deep into his eyes. They were still blue. They still crinkled at the edges. But it didn't matter anymore. Even though he was real, even though I was wide awake, I understood that Stan was only a dream. I sighed. It's always hard to wake up.

"I don't think Sarah likes snakes," I said.

That's when we heard the first scream. We started back at a run. Then came the second.

Eventually, Sarah had gotten tired of watching the women. Most of the kids had gone on the hayride. Finding nothing else to do, Sarah wandered down among the vehicles. When she came to Stan's Jeep, the last in the line, she recognized it from my descriptions. Its top was down, and the back was full of his equipment. Sarah is curious. She wanted to see what kind of equipment a field biologist would use for studying wildflowers and butterflies. So she started poking around.

As she was doing this, the hay wagon full of kids was coming up the last stretch of Minnie Berry's road. Rick was driving Gabriel all by himself, because Ben and Jordy were back in the hay with the other kids. Actually, they were under the hay. Ben had discovered necking.

As the wagon drew up close to the Jeep, Rick waved at Sarah. Sarah, who had just picked up an interesting-looking white bag that seemed to be moving slightly, waved back. Then she opened the drawstring top and looked in. She screamed. And dropped the bag.

Sarah's scream startled Gabriel, who had been on edge all day anyway. He bolted. Rick pulled back on the reins with all his might, but wasn't strong enough to stop him. The wagon jolted into a hole, and Ben and Jordy, who'd been at the very back, rolled to the edge. The wagon lurched out of the hole and Jordy went over. She cracked her head on a rock and lay still. The wagon kept going.

That's when Sarah screamed again. A very frightened, very angry rattlesnake, having wriggled free of the bag, was crawling toward Jordy, its head weaving back and forth, its tongue flicking. Dazed, Jordy started to sit up.

"Don't move!" Dad yelled. Sarah's first scream had wakened him, and he had come running as fast as his ankle would allow to see what was going on. "Don't move," he said again.

The snake, its rattle vibrating ominously, was closing in on Jordy's legs. Dad had no time to think. He simply lunged forward and, with his left hand, grabbed that timber rattler at the base of its skull and held on, while the body whipped and coiled itself around his arm.

Sarah, sobbing now, snatched up the bag and, with more nerve than she knew she had, held it open while Dad stuck the snake down inside. "On the count of three," Dad said. "One, two, *three!*"

He let go, pulled his hand out, and Sarah pulled the drawstring closed.

That's when Stan and I arrived. And nearly everybody else.

Instantly Dad became a hero. Jordy's father, once he'd made sure Jordy was all right, clapped Dad on the back and practically shook his left hand off. The other men clustered around, offering congratulations. No longer an outsider, Dad had been suddenly accepted into the ranks of mountain men. A man who, in spite of his injuries, was willing to tackle a timber rattler with one bare hand. Who cared about porches?

Sarah was a hero, too, of course, when she finally stopped crying. "I don't know how I did that," she said, "but it was the bravest thing I've ever done."

Stan put Number Thirty-one safely back into his Jeep, in a locked specimen box this time, and thanked Dad. "That was wonderful," he said. "Someone else might have killed her. Endangered species or not."

Ben and Jordy went off somewhere to let Jordy rest and recover from her near catastrophe. Rick put Gabriel back in his barn and gave him a carrot to soothe his nerves.

Dad, his limp amazingly improved, was ushered to Minnie Berry's best rocking chair. Mom brought him a huge dish of peach ice cream. Sarah and I had some, too.

A little while later, when the porch was finished, Jacques Gagnon called for square dancing. Marcia, awake and well by that time, was standing on the new porch when the call went up for a fiddle. "Fiddle?" she asked. "Do you mean violin?"

"They mean fiddle," Minnie Berry said, and went inside. Moments later she was back, carrying a gleaming violin and a bow. "Jacques made this one for me himself!"

Marcia's eyes almost popped out of her head. And when Miss Berry started to play, Marcia's jaw dropped open. Minnie Berry was terrific. The Gagnons organized the dancing, and Mom sent Rick back to *Brunhilda* to get Marcia's violin. When the square dancers finally quit in exhaustion, Marcia and Minnie Berry retired inside for a session that Mom later called "dueling fiddles."

Minnie Berry had made me a surprise birthday cake, which was served with the rest of the peach ice cream. Everybody sang to me. And asked, of course, how old I was.

When I said sixteen, Stan's face went pale under his tan. "Sixteen? Today?"

"Sweet sixteen and never been kissed," Sarah said solemnly.

Stan leaned over and kissed me on the forehead. "There. That should take care of that." He ran his hand through his gorgeous sandy hair. "Well, I'd better be getting to the lab," he said. He did not ask me to go with him.

"I hope Number Thirty-one's okay." I really meant it.

"I'm sure she'll be fine."

And then he was gone. Freckles, beard stubble, biceps, and all. It was okay. Jason, I thought, would be there when I got back to the city. Good old Jason. He'd have beard stubble, too, someday.

I did tell Jason about Stan later, by the way. After he'd told me about Isabelle!

After all the people had gathered their dishes and their tools and their children and roared away in their four-wheel-drive cars and trucks, Miss Berry and Jacques Gagnon called us into the cabin. They stood side by side, and we squeezed around the table, especially crowded since Sarah and Jordy were both there with us. Miss Berry was holding a bottle, and there was a row of glasses lined up in front of us.

"My best raspberry wine," she said, pouring a little red liquid into each glass. "I want to thank you all." She smiled at Jacques Gagnon, and he smiled back at her. "I've learned something very important from you Skinners."

"You learned from *us*?" Marcia asked.

"The best teachers are always ready to learn, young lady. Remember that!"

"What did you learn?" This was Rick.

"Maybe it wasn't learning so much as remembering something I'd forgotten," Miss Berry said. She gave a glass to Jacques Gagnon and took one herself. "I'd like to propose a toast."

We each picked up a glass, even Rick, who waited till Mom nodded.

"Here's to family. And sharing."

We clinked glasses all around and took a sip. The wine was light and sweet and warm in the back of the throat.

Mr. Gagnon held his glass up then. "Here's to marriage," he said.

We all just looked at him. He smiled. "Miss Minnie Berry has finally agreed to become Mrs. Jacques Gagnon."

Miss Berry explained that Mr. Gagnon had been trying

to get her to say yes for twenty years, but she'd always refused. She'd hated to lose her independence. "And besides, he was too young. Didn't want people to think I was robbing the cradle." She looked at his white hair and mustache. "Not much danger of that now."

The festivities were interrupted by Lucifer barking outside. Dad, who was closest to the door, went to see what he was barking at. "Ye gods!" he yelled. Buffy came up the steps and onto the porch. There wasn't any doubt about what had happened. Buffy had been skunked.

So my birthday wasn't perfect. As you mature, you learn that nothing is.

.... Epilogue ....

No matter what you may have heard, tomato juice does not completely get rid of skunk smell on a dog. Nothing does. Buffy had to spend the next week outside. On a chain, in case there were any other skunks lurking nearby.

Sarah survived her remaining few days in the wilderness, and Quasimodo got her safely back to Lower Stag to catch her bus. She said she'd learned a lot, but from what I could see, the mountains hadn't really changed her. She went home in the sundress we'd washed at the Laundromat, wearing stockings and heels, lipstick, eye shadow, and nail polish. "In the civilized world," she said, "appearance counts!"

Our last weeks in the mountains were terrific. The weather cooperated, giving us warm sunny days and cold, starry nights. We worked hard, of course, but we played, too. This was vacation, after all. A beautiful, educational, exhausting vacation.

Mom finished her series of columns on homesteading. She wrote that while the challenges could be invigorating, and meeting them could give one a great sense of personal accomplishment, most people should take the wilderness in small doses.

After he'd arranged to have *Brunhilda* towed home, Dad called a family meeting to say that with the fireplace at home for warmth, all we needed was to buy a couple of kerosene lamps and keep a propane stove in the garage, to be ready for whatever minor collapse might befall civilization in the near future. Perhaps, he added, we would buy a portable generator.

In one of the most blatant turnarounds in Skinner history, Marcia hated to leave Minnie Berry. She had started writing a report called "Mountain Woman" and was learning to fiddle. "Madame Ardelle will be blown away when I go back to my violin lessons," she said, ripping through "Turkey in the Straw." We were sure she was right.

Rick wanted to take Gabriel back with us. "He could live in the garage," he suggested. Mom told him that Miss Berry would miss the mule terribly, and he finally agreed that Gabriel should stay.

As September approached, Dad thought up the perfect revenge to wreak on Henry. He would offer to take Quasimodo off Henry's hands. "He wouldn't dare ask more than a pittance. It barely runs." Then, he would take it home, restore it, and drive it into Stag the next summer in pristine glory, painted, shining, and incredibly valuable.

Henry did dare to ask more than a pittance, but once Dad has taken hold of an idea, he's hard to shake. Quasimodo was ours.

Unlike Sarah, Czar Nicholas was permanently changed by the great north woods. In his old age he had become a dedicated mouser. He never went after anything bigger, but with mice, he was a demon. I guess Rick had changed, too. He forgave him. "It's just nature," he explained.

As it turned out, we did sort of take Caliban home with us. Chatter was pregnant. When her litter arrived, there was one Caliban and two Chatter-Caliban mixes. We took her to the vet shortly afterward to be sure she didn't surprise us that way again, and gave two of the kittens to the kid who had taken care of Rick's rats. Marcia kept the female mix for her own, as a symbol of the blending of wilderness and civilization, and named her Minnie.

Ben was the only one who really hated leaving the mountains. Nothing, not the prospect of varsity soccer or the workshop that waited for him at home—not even his computer—could compete with Jordy. She promised to write, and he was invited to come up to the Gagnons' for Thanksgiving. It was the best anybody could do. Adolescence is tough.

Minnie Berry and Jacques Gagnon set their wedding date in October. "You can come for the wedding and the autumn leaves at the same time," she said. She was planning to move to the next valley with Mr. Gagnon for the winter, but they'd both come live in her log cabin next summer. "So he can help with the garden. Unless you all want to come back." We politely declined.

As for me, I was glad to come home. Glad for bathtubs and washing machines and unlimited hot water. I don't take them for granted anymore—homesteading really did do that. I'm just very glad to have them. Also Jason, who has never so much as mentioned rattlesnakes.

I have my key to Quasimodo, but dreams die hard. I still think of that red BMW. With automatic transmission.